A FALLING

Scott Carlin

First published in 2022 by Blossom Spring Publishing
A Falling Of Snow
Copyright © 2022 Scott Carlin
ISBN 978-1-7391561-2-1
E: admin@blossomspringpublishing.com
W: www.blossomspringpublishing.com
Published in the United Kingdom. All rights reserved under
International Copyright Law. Contents and/or cover may not be
reproduced in whole or in part without the express written consent of
the publisher.
This is a work of fiction. Names, characters, places and incidents
are either products of the author's imagination or are used
fictitiously.

For my dad, Peter, who never quite managed to finish it,
this is dedicated to you.

Chapter 1

The sky was threatening, as if at any moment it would fall, engulfing everything and everyone. It was forecast to snow but as of yet, it had relented.

Ryan was standing at the meeting point given to him by his handler. He was leaning against a lamp post; hands in his pockets and coat collar turned up, about twenty feet from the entrance of one of the many arch bridges in Edinburgh's old town. The wind coming through it, was less than pleasant. It was ten past ten at night and the city streets were quiet. Ryan was staring, through the vapour of his own breath, at the top of an old-style Victorian lamp post across the street. It was similar to the one above 221b Baker Street, he thought. He imagined if he climbed up there, he would be able to touch the clouds as they were so low. His next thought was that the cold may be having an effect on his mind.

The secure email he'd received just before seven that night had instructed him where and when he was to meet his handler. The fact the meeting was to be on the same day told him the matter at hand was either very delicate or very important, or both. Since his last case had been only a week ago, it was also a little unexpected.

Just as he thought about moving further away from the bridge, he heard the sound of a diesel engine working hard against the cold before he saw it. Then, with its lights dipping and flickering against the wall behind him as it came over the bow of the hill, the car came into view. It took Ryan a split second to know this was not his contact. The car was similar, but there was a passenger inside. With some disappointment he averted his gaze to the icy pavement below.

Just thirty seconds later, a second car appeared over

the hill and rumbled along the cobbled road before coming to a halt halfway into the tunnel opposite. Ryan waited for the reverse lights to come on, as had been the agreed signal. After a few seconds he pushed himself off the lamp post, fastened his top button and straightened his collar against the wind. Checking the road in both directions, he crossed and moments later he was in the passenger seat of the BMW, very thankful for its German engineered heated leather seats.

The contact's name was Jones. He hadn't been on the job long from what Ryan knew. He had seen him only once before a few months back, running errands on a job in Oslo. A decent enough guy from what he had heard. Competent and eager, spoke when required.

'Cold one,' Ryan said.

'Yeah. You been waiting long?'

'About an hour. Could've been worse. What you got for me?'

'File is here. It's a job in Europe as far as we know. Pretty vague to be honest, just came through this afternoon. Where and when is all, it tells us.'

Ryan took the file and opened it up as Jones put the car into first gear and pulled away. They turned first left then left again onto Princes Street, crossed the North Bridge, and came to a halt at the foot of the Royal Mile. Ryan shook Jones' hand before getting out without speaking.

After a short uphill walk, he entered a café and found a table by the window, giving him a view of the famous street outside. He ordered a pot of tea from a rather tired looking middle-aged man; Ryan opened the file and began reading. Jones had been right. It was pretty vague. Tomorrow morning, he was to take the 07.45 flight from Edinburgh to Schiphol airport, Amsterdam, then make his way to the Krasnapolsky Hotel and wait for further instructions.

Ryan sat for another twenty minutes watching the flow of tourists milling up and down the famous street. He wasn't sure where he'd been born but he'd always regarded Edinburgh as his home. He paid his bill and made his way out into the cold night heading for his apartment. He wandered through the old streets, up the Royal Mile before turning left onto the Grassmarket. There was the usual buzz from the pubs with groups of people heading in and out. Ryan watched with a tinge of envy. He loved his job, the places it took him and all it entailed, but he had missed out on much of the normal socialising of a man in his youth, because of it.

He continued on to Princes Gardens, crossed the Waverly Street bridge past the station, before arriving at his apartment on Princes Street. He rode the elevator up to his flat and, once inside, took off his hat and coat before slumping on to the sofa. He checked his watch, aware that he would need to be at the airport early in the morning but, before he had finished the thought, his eyes began to close and he fell asleep, still fully dressed.

***

Early next morning, Ryan was on a tram heading for the airport. He had bought a tea and a newspaper and was halfway through both by the time he got off at terminal two. As he walked through the main entrance, the digital clock read 6:41 and showed the temperature to be minus three. While on the tram, he had overheard a passenger say it was too cold for snow, which was a myth he had never really understood.

The airport felt big and cold and empty. He always felt uneasy in airports, perhaps due to the nature of his work. He went to his designated locker, number four.

Inside he found a passport and a smartphone. He turned the phone on, put the passport in his coat pocket, and made his way to check-in. He had brought only a small bag as hand luggage which he could carry onto the plane and, hopefully avoid delays. After checking in, he ordered a cooked breakfast in one of the many airport cafés. As he ate, he pretended to read his paper while keeping an eye out for a face in the crowd which didn't look quite right.

When his flight was called, he paid his bill and ordered a coffee to go. Another caffeine hit was always helpful this early in the morning. When he finally got to the door of the plane, the steward directed him to first-class. This would never be Ryan's first choice but it had been booked for him, so he wasn't going to argue. He was aboard a Boeing 757, which he had travelled in many times, and first-class offered more than anyone could need. It had comfortable seats, plenty of leg room and even the offer of a pre-flight drink which, on this occasion, Ryan declined. He settled in and got ready for take-off as the third trigger went off in his head and he knew things were not going as planned.

Chapter 2

Four hundred miles away things were going exactly to plan, as they usually did. Ryan's old unit had landed in Amsterdam twenty-four hours prior to the meeting. The four-man team hit Amsterdam Central Station at 9:25 and by 9:55 they were checking in to a local hotel just off the main road.

First, they scanned the Main Street to identify two lookout points where they would be close enough to see everything but not too close so as to be noticeable. This was never easy in these circumstances, so appropriate time was taken. The key was to be invisible while in plain sight, act naturally and appear to have a believable reason for standing in the same place for a couple of hours. Giving even the most observant passers-by no reason to be suspicious. These guys had done this a thousand times though and knew how it went. They would be able to spot trouble anywhere within three hundred yards.

The second task was to find a café or a bar across the street from the meeting point. It should have a table seat with a clear view and easy access to the front door. Good coffee was a bonus. The third guy would be running the operation from here. In everyone's ear, calling the game.

The third and final preparation was to scour the streets surrounding the main building. Every doorway, alleyway, and backstreet. Anywhere someone could get in, or out. Things can go wrong and being able to escape a tight situation when needed can save lives.

The fourth man would be at the meeting but not that anyone would know. He would be incognito, invisible and alert. There may be others with an interest in proceedings, so it was too risky to deploy bugs or other detectable tech. He would need to rely solely on his specialist training — always an operative's most potent weapon.

After completing the setup, triple checking every detail, they split into pairs and began a four-hour shift rota. One pair ate and slept, while the other ran through the whole routine again.

***

Back on the runway, Ryan was running the same routine in his head. Back to front, front to back. It was the same routine he had run himself many times before, and not as long ago as he would have liked to remember.

Chapter 3

Training is important, experience invaluable. When both are combined, and applied to the right mind, they can make the un-noticeable, noticeable. Thus, Ryan's subconscious had detected a pattern in recent events and set off a trigger that would put him on red alert.

First, it had been the man checking his boarding card. He had mistakenly handed him the ticket upside down, with his finger covering his name, yet he called his name out before he had looked at it. It was only a split second and might not have been noticed, but now it seemed obvious.

Then there was the stewardess. She had directed him to first class even though his boarding card had remained in his top pocket. She should not have known. Was it maybe being a little overanxious on her part? Or did he just look like the first-class type? Probably not, he decided.

There was one more thing. It had been part of the protocol from his old unit that, before boarding any flight, they should check the flight status and the available seats on it. It's always useful to know what room you have on the plane, and what you might need to deal with if a 'situation' should occur. Also, it can help you to discover if someone may be following you.

When Ryan checked the status five minutes prior to boarding, it showed four seats in first class that were taken and four still available. Nothing unusual for an ordinary flight. Two minutes after fastening his seat belt though, he saw that first class was full to capacity, not with bestseller carrying tourists, but with the type of men that he had worked with his whole life. He knew the situation had changed the moment the third man had taken his seat. He had to adjust, work out a plan. He reached up and hit the service button.

'Think I'll take that drink after all,' he told the stewardess.

'Certainly sir, what can I get you?'

'A bottle of water, please.'

'Certainly sir, be right back.'

She returned shortly after with a sealed bottle and a napkin. His mouth was getting dry and he tried to open the bottle but he didn't have the strength, he tried to stay calm. He settled into his seat, all the time watching the four new 'holidaymakers'. Not one of them moved, asked for anything, or even spoke to each other. They were all patiently waiting, undoubtedly feeling the same tingle of adrenalin he was. It stayed this way for close to ten minutes. A weird kind of atmosphere was building, getting more and more tense, but still no one spoke, or moved.

This is when Ryan began to feel strange. His head felt hazy and his eyes heavy. But it wasn't tiredness, more like getting hit by a ton of bricks. He tried to fight it but was powerless. He felt his heart begin to race, sweat on his forehead, and the whole plane was spinning. He tried to stand as discreetly as he could, but his legs felt like jelly. He fell back into his seat. He knew he was going under. His eyelids felt like cannonballs. He tried to slow his breathing and fastened his seat belt again. No point resisting now, just close your eyes and hope for the best.

It was then, just seconds before he finally passed out, that he realised the biggest mistake he had missed. The second cup of coffee he had bought at the airport café. It had been poured behind the counter, out of sight for just a second. And that second had caught him out.

'Damn,' he thought, as he fought the inevitable. He could see her face. The woman from the airport café, who had served him his eggs and bacon. The same woman who had just handed him the bottle of water and the napkin.

Chapter 4

Ryan woke with a jump, heart still racing and drenched in sweat, he felt like he had been out for days. He stood up, stretched, and rubbed his eyes, he could feel the blood rushing back to his legs and head again. Things slowly started coming back to him. He looked round the cabin, it was empty. The aircrafts main door was open and letting cold air out and a ray of winter light into the cabin, it was hurting his eyes as he slowly walked towards it. There were no oxygen masks hanging from above the seats, it looked like a plane waiting to be boarded.

'You're awake.'

Her voice was like a drill going in one ear but not out the other, she was one of the cabin crew, she had come bouncing through the door just as he reached it.

'What the hell is happening?' he asked disorientated.

Ryan recognised her from the flight, she came into first class a few times during the flight, but mostly served in economy, she wasn't the one that had served him the eggs, six inches too small, different hair colour, born in a different generation.

'I'm not quite sure,' she was panting as she spoke.

'How long have I been out?'

The look of fear and confusion on her face told him she had as much of a clue about what was going on, as he did.

'I have been trying to wake you for the last ten minutes.'

He glanced out the side window and could see the plane was still a good distance from the main terminal, he couldn't see any passengers, which meant they had made it inside already. There was a frost on the grass at the side of the runway, so he knew it was still morning, as the temperature had not got high enough to thaw it out.

'What time is it now?' he said.

'9:32,' she replied.

'I don't understand, why are we still sitting on the runway?'

'To be honest I'm not quite sure, it's all been a bit crazy. We landed as normal but shortly afterwards the captain announced that there would be a short delay as a departing flight had been delayed.'

Ryan still felt lightheaded.

'After five minutes of not moving the captain came on again to say that there'd be another ten-minute delay before the gate would be clear and that was when it all started; four men from first class got up and began telling people that the plane had a problem and wasn't safe and they all had to get out quickly.'

Things began to make sense now, Ryan had thought that the four men on the plane were there for him, which was a little flattering, but now his thoughts were that they probably wouldn't have been aware of him, not until they tried to wake him to get off the plane, and if he could spot them, then they could spot him. The stewardess on the plane was most likely the one who was sent to delay him, and a good job she had done, he never realised until it was too late.

The men had then reacted quickly and effectively. Ryan knew they must be heading to Amsterdam for the same reason that he was, they either missed a previous flight or got the call for the job even later than he had. His main problem now was that they were at least fifteen minutes ahead of him and almost certainly going to the same location as he was.

'Just before we turned for the terminal, one of the men said that they thought you were armed and not to let you off.'

'Damn.' Ryan said to himself.

Once they had realised who he was, they would have assumed that he was heading to the same location as they were, and this was the ideal way to delay him.

His main problem now was that he had to get the hell off this plane, and fast.

Chapter 5

It was a clever decoy, especially at short notice. These guys would fly through the airport and be heading for the city in no time.

Ryan knew the only chance to get out quick was to head for the terminal, the perimeter fence was ten-foot-high though, and about three miles round, probably closer to fifteen feet standing next to it.

Ryan stepped of the evacuation chute and decided his best option was to head for the terminal building. When he hit the tarmac, he started running at full speed until he reached an emergency door at the bottom of the main terminal, it opened easily with one good kick, the thing that Ryan wasn't expecting though was that it set of an alarm. He had to hurry, he took a flight of stairs that brought him out into what appeared to be, a large canteen, lockers on one side, a few cupboards and a sink on the other. There were random chairs scattered everywhere, it was empty.

There were no windows, just another door. He opened it just enough to see out, a group of workers were gathered with their backs to him at what must be a meeting point if the alarm sounded, they all had orange safety uniforms on. Ryan closed the door and found a vest hanging on a hook behind it, he put it on and slipped out the room. No one moved as he crept past, they were all staring out the window at the plane abandoned on the runway.

Ryan passed around the outside of them and headed for the only door he could see that would take him out to the airport terminal floor. From a window he could see it led to the baggage claim, not that he had any now, but it was his only exit.

He got there quickly and quietly, with his vest on and

his head down and made for the airport train station, and if he was right, even with the alarm, they would still be running a service out of the airport.

The main entrance to the airport was packed, people pushing and shoving their way to the exits, the tannoy was telling them to do so, first in Dutch, then English.

Ryan fought his way through the crowds and reached the escalators in the middle of the floor. The railway for Schiphol was directly under the airport building, it ran in four different lines, the main one taking you to Amsterdam central, which was the one he needed.

The escalators themselves were empty, he assumed people thought the trains would be cancelled due to the alarm sounding but, in an evacuation, anything taking you from a possible emergency would still be operating.

Ryan reached the station floor, there was nobody about apart from two policemen waiting at the entrance. They were too busy talking to each other to notice him coming in, the train was waiting and ready to leave, he nodded to the first man as he approached them, all he got was a lazy smile in return.

The train was maybe half full. Ryan stood at the far end to keep a good view of the whole carriage and prayed for the driver to depart. If there were no more delays he thought, he could hit the city Centre the same time as his friends from the plane.

***

The four men from the flight had jumped into a blacked-out jeep when they exited the airport, but they were still twenty minutes from Amsterdam and the traffic on the A4 ring road was heavy. It was now just after ten in the morning and the roads were getting busier by the minute.

The team had received a call since landing telling

them what the job was, it seemed reasonably straight forward, they were to grab their target from a café in the centre of Amsterdam and get him out as quickly and quietly as possible. They knew a smash and grab was never easy or quiet but with four of them they could more than manage.

Ryan's worry was that there were now at least two teams involved, and he was still standing fifteen minutes outside of where he should have been half an hour ago.

Chapter 6

The train felt like it was taking forever, the fact that they stopped at every station on the route wasn't helping. The majority of people would be heading for the city Centre the same as Ryan, he thought. There still hadn't been any contact from his handler since yesterday afternoon and Ryan still didn't know the plan after reaching the hotel.

As the train approached central station most of the travelers in the carriage began heading for the doors, Ryan was aware of a group of people talking behind him about what they thought was the incident at the airport, of a man on board a plane with a gun.

The train finally stopped, and the people pushed out onto the platform, Ryan threw the vest into the bin on the train as he passed it, he hoped he was just another face in the crowd.

Amsterdam central train station sees around 170.000 people on an average day, and it felt like they were all here at this exact moment as Ryan made his way out. The station was made up of two sections, the old run-down section that greeted you as you came up from the platform, then the new commercial section. Ryan could see at least three coffee shops, two bars and two restaurants inside it.

He reached the main entrance and came out into the bitter cold that was Amsterdam City Centre, and quickly headed for Dam square. The streets were as busy as the station had been. Tourists standing in groups looking at maps, along with all types of workers busying between them, no doubt heading to offices and shops to begin their working day.

Ryan was walking down the city's main street; it was clear the majority of tourists were heading in the same direction. The right-hand side of the street was a combination of pubs, cafés, and souvenir shops, paying top dollar no doubt to get the first of the tourist's money. The famous Amsterdam canal was on his left, boats were all lined up ready for their days trade.

Ryan slowed and checked his phone, still no message, he wasn't quite sure how to proceed without instruction. He put his now freezing hands into his pockets to heat them and found a folded piece of paper inside that read.

'Grand hotel Krasnapolsky, room 44, equipment already there, gather as much info as possible from a meeting taking place at a café across the street'.

When the hell was that put there, he thought. This meant that either his boss, or handler must be here in the city also, but he couldn't be sure. Ryan had been in the job just over four years and he still hadn't met him, when he thought about it, he had never actually spoke to him.

Ryan knew that the Krasnapolsky sat at the bottom of the road he was currently on but thought better of continuing on it. So instead, he doubled back fifty yards onto Oudebrugsteeg that crossed over the canal and came out in the middle of Warmoesstraat, the red-light districts main street, which was quiet at this hour. He took a right and followed it to the end, which put him directly behind the hotel.

He knew from previous experience that lookouts would be at the front of the hotel, but he would be surprised if there were any on the back street. From entering through a rear door, he should be able to get to his room unseen and on time. He checked his watch 10:09 a.m. he could still make it assuming there were no more delays.

Chapter 7

The blacked-out jeep was through the worst of the traffic. It had turned off the A10 and was now on the S112 Wibautstraat road which runs directly into the city Centre.

The driver had the heavy car working it's twenty-inch tyres, switching lanes, pushing it as hard as he could, they were still at least five minutes behind, and their schedule was blown. Regardless of their instructions now the smash and grab was all they had left, it was going to be loud, it was going to be fast, and it was going to happen in the next five minutes.

***

Ryan found a door at the rear entrance of the hotel; it appeared to be an access door for workers as there was no handle on the outside but luckily it was wedged open slightly. He could smell hot food cooking as he pulled it open and stepped inside.

It took him into a kitchen area, not too big and with very little inside, a stove was heating a pot of soup which gave the smell. Ryan passed through quickly and out a door at the far end of the room which brought him out at the end of the hotel's main foyer, it was impressive looking to say the least, old fashioned but in an elegant way. A chandelier hung above the reception and drew your eye the second you stepped in. The hotel was busy with people checking in or out, could be either, at this time of the morning.

Ryan composed himself, straightened his jacket and ran a hand through his hair. He concentrated on slowing his breathing, a panting madman usually draws attention in a hotel such as this, or any hotel for that matter. The room key was waiting for him, his room was on the fourth floor so he headed for the stairs, it would be much quicker than waiting on a lift.

He swiped his key card and entered what was a standard European city Centre hotel. A mixture of cosy and modern yet still in theme with the hotel. It was a nice room with a large bathroom, shower on the right, a huge double bed taking up most of the space, and on the far side there was a bedside table with an alarm clock, in the corner was a well-used armchair. His rifle was sitting between the two of them already set up and pointing out between a set of velvet curtains.

The TV was on when Ryan came in, but all the lights were out. He did a quick sweep of the room, it was clean. He checked the clock 10:14 a.m. perfect timing he said to himself with a sigh of relief. A letter lying on the bed addressed to Dr Kerlin caught his eye, he lifted it and put it in his coat pocket for later.

The gun was cold under his arm, he hadn't used it in a while, but it felt as good as ever. He nestled it in against his shoulder and checked the clock again, 10:15 a.m. he smiled and put his eye to the scope.

The curtain hid the gun well from the outside world. It was set pointing directly at a café across the main street from the hotel, and on the corner of Dam square. He had a great vantage point of its front window. He held his breath and waited, nothing else to do now but wait, the last twelve hours had flown by, and he knew nothing would change anytime soon.

Chapter 8

The sun was beginning to break through the morning mist and Dam square was starting to fill with people. The street performers were out and standing in front of the palace grounds in their costumes ready to make a day's living, groups of tourists were swarming around them.

The café where the meeting was taking place was on the ground floor of an old tenement building, the three floors above belonged to a budget hotel chain.

Through the lens Ryan could see what he assumed was the meeting he was there to witness, there were two men sitting at a table. He had assumed there would be more, he wasn't sure why. The man he had a clear sight off was sitting against the back wall, he looked in his late forties, medium build, light brown hair, and a mustache that added five years to him. The second man was sitting directly across the table from him. From what Ryan could make out he looked a few inches taller with jet black hair, he wasn't carrying as much weight either, but it was difficult to tell from the angle Ryan had on him. They looked like they had been sitting for a few minutes already as they both had coffees in front of them, the one with the mustache was doing most of the talking and all in all, it looked like a casual conversation.

It continued like this for the next five minutes and Ryan began to doubt that he was looking at the meeting that he was here for. People were coming in and out of the café as normal, some passing by or stopping to look in and make a decision. The two men's conversation continued all the same.

Ryan took the opportunity to try and spot the lookouts and what he might need to deal with should he have to break cover. The first one he picked out with relative ease, he was fifty yards up from the café on the other side of the street, standing outside a souvenir shop. He was easily six foot five, not the biggest shoulders but certainly not to be messed with, he was wearing a hat that covered what was surely a shaved head, the face would definitely have suited it anyway. Dressed all in black as he expected, trousers and trench coat with proper military boots, the boots always gave them away. The earpiece was barely visible to Ryan in the few times that the guy faced his way, with the help of the scope of course.

The second man would be underneath Ryan and to the left, looking at the café from the south. He would be slightly farther away than the first but with a better angle. Ryan also didn't imagine him being any different in appearance to the first man. They come out the factory like that, he thought to himself.

Ryan focused on the café window again and after a minute one of the men, the one he could not see very well, got up from the table and headed further inside the café. There had been no farewell handshake, so Ryan assumed it was a toilet break, which seemed pretty strange considering the circumstances. After only a few minutes the man with the jet-black hair returned to the table but he wasn't alone, there was another man with him who sat at the table between the two. He was easily a decade younger than the other two men at the meeting and slim. He was wearing an expensive suit, clean shaved and had an expensive haircut, it was hard to make out if he was meant to be there, but the conversation certainly seemed to have changed and was starting to become heated, more facial expressions and hand gestures.

Ryan glanced at the clock 10:24, he returned to the scope just in time to see the man with the moustache stand up from the table, his chair flying back as he did. The slim guy in the suit stood up and tried to calm him down but it wasn't hard to see that he was way past that, he was bordering on furious and was now being held back from jumping the table to reach the man with the jet-black hair. It was turning into a bar fight as all three men were on their feet and pulling and grabbing at each other. Just as it was breaking into a riot, something far off in the distance caught Ryan's ear.

Chapter 9

The noise Ryan heard was the sound of an engine at full tilt and the squeal of tyres turning at speeds they weren't really designed for. The blacked-out jeep was moving fast and wasn't all that far away. The chaos in the café was still escalating when the jeep skidded to a halt right outside and before anyone could react, there were three passengers from Ryan's flight this morning, bursting out of the car and heading inside while a fourth stood at the door facing out onto the street. From what Ryan could make out none of them had guns drawn but he had no doubt they would be armed.

He had to assess the situation and think quick. His only two options were to either stay put and gather as much information as he could from the mayhem that was taking place in front of him, or head for the street. He knew he could be down to it in ninety seconds if he took the stairs but by that time whatever was happening, could be over.

He decided to stay and watch as this had been his instructions. Through the lens was now a commotion of bodies, most of them dressed in black which also wasn't helping. After only a minute the scene spilled out onto the street. The three men who had entered were now heading back to the jeep, with the man with the jet-black hair now in tow. He was being dragged, showing restrain but all the while knowing it was futile. He was younger than Ryan had initially thought, maybe early fifties, the jet-black hair was also a full head worth. He looked important and well dressed, especially for where he was heading to, Ryan thought. They bundled him into the jeep and sped away, the fourth guy slamming the door as they left. Taking out the back tyre with his rifle crossed Ryan's mind, but he still wasn't entirely sure his job in all this, and he didn't want to draw any unnecessary attention to himself.

When the jeep was out of sight Ryan returned his attention to the café. There was now a crowd of people gathered at the front window but still no faces he could recognise. Police sirens were beginning to sound off in the distance.

He watched for a few more minutes before deciding to head down to the street and have a closer look. He was just about to pack up when he saw a face, he did recognise. It was the third mystery man from the meeting, he came out of an alleyway next to the café and turned left. Ryan assumed, heading for the station.

Ryan left the rifle as he found it and headed for the stairs, eighty-four seconds later he was on the Damrak and running for the station. He had to at least know where the man was heading for even if he didn't catch him, it might be the only decent information he would gather from the job.

Ryan finally caught sight of him, heading through the main doors of central station. He scrambled through the crowds, pushing and throwing people out of his way. He caught another glimpse as he headed down the stairs to platform five. Ryan followed as best he could but was still thirty yards behind.

When they reached the platform, they both jumped the gate, Ryan took the stairs three at a time and as he hit the platform floor, he saw the train doors begin to close.

'Hold that train!' Ryan screamed, turning everyone on the platform around to face him.

He was too late; it had begun departing.

He got to the front of the platform as it started to speed up, the information board on the side of it said direct to Dortmund. Ryan stood for a second in a daze, trying his best to see the face of the man he had chased, on the train. It was useless, there was too many people. He turned and started checking faces as they headed out to the terminal, after all he never actually saw him board the train. He ran the full length of the platform again, checking with one eye still on the train, everyone was almost out — he definitely wasn't here.

The train was almost gone, this was his only lead, and it was looking like he had lost it, he was the only one left on the platform as he headed for the exit.

He approached the steps and glanced at the last carriage as it headed into the tunnel. It had picked up speed and was moving fast now. It was completely empty, except for a lone figure standing at the back window, this figure was staring out at him. It was the man he had been chasing, he *had* got on the train.

Ryan stopped dead and stared hard, remembering the face as best he could. He might not see it again for a while, but he *would* see it again, he would make sure of it.

The final image he had of the figure as the train disappeared into the tunnel was of a young man with a broad, smug smile spread across a slim pale face that was looking straight at him.

Ryan turned to the stairs in front of him, remembering the face. He took a moment before heading up and out onto the cold city street.

Chapter 10

The jeep had sped away from the café seconds after screeching to a halt, it wasn't a world record time by their standards, but still competent. They had expected a little more resistance from inside, but it went smoothly. The big guy with the shaved head sitting in the passenger seat was on the phone to his unit's boss, who was still sitting in the bar across the street from the café, he was letting him know that all had went well and to see if they got away clean with no one tailing them, the man in the café said that they had.

When he ended the call, he told the driver to head to the car park as normal. They were stopping at a golf club just outside Amsterdam, where they would swap their car for a Volvo 4x4 that had been stolen the day before. From there they would move onto the base which was an old bread factory on the outskirts of a town called Nieuwpoort, it was situated 6 miles south of the city Centre and far enough out to stay hidden. The team had used the factory a few times before and were happy enough that it wasn't compromised. The plan was to wait it out for at least 48 hours before being told of an extraction point — where they would then move their target onto.

It took them twenty-five minutes to reach the factory, they had been driving at a normal speed, so as not to attract any unwanted attention. They drove through the town of Nieuwpoort slowly, looking around, there wasn't really much to it. They turned off the main road and onto a country road that led to the factory. They approached slowly as the large aluminum shutter door opened and the 4x4 drove through. It closed quickly behind them, and they all got out, dragging the package with them. He hadn't said a word on the journey from the café and grunted as he was pushed into his room — the door locked behind him.

The old team Ryan used to be part of was every bit as good and every bit as competent as the one he was part of now, the only difference was their moral scales tipped slightly towards the corrupt end. For instance, he knew that if certain information could be obtained, or if a person could be blackmailed then there was usually a bigger financial gain, certainly more than working for a legitimate organisation like the British government. Ryan did have an idea after a while that this was going on back when he was part of the unit, and their agenda was almost never for the good of their country.

Once he had realised who he was working with, it took a lot of work and people in the right places to make the switch to his new unit happen.

Chapter 11

Ryan was now officially lost. He walked out of the station but this time not towards the main street. He turned left and followed a ring road that ran around the city Centre.

He was going through the last forty minutes in his head trying to pinpoint something that stood out, or something useful that he could take from the café. He walked for nearly an hour before finding a bar that seemed relatively quiet. He sat by the window and ordered a beer, took out his smartphone and tried to call head office with no reply. He put the phone back in his pocket and remembered the envelope from the hotel room, he opened it and read what was his next meeting point.

'Sunday 22nd, Amsterdam arena, Ajax v Volendam — kick off at 12:30pm, ticket enclosed.'

He had never de-briefed at a football match before and even if this was the purpose of the meeting, he knew he didn't have that much to de-brief on. His boss must also be taking security very seriously to be meeting at a football stadium which he assumed would probably be full to capacity.

He took out his phone again, checked train times for the next morning and the layout of the stadium. He knew little but was still wanting to be there on time and give his best account and hopefully get some more information on the job.

The waitress appeared next to him — he asked for another beer, he didn't have anywhere else to be that he knew off so why not. As she left and headed to the bar, he heard a voice telling the waitress to make it two. He turned in his seat towards the door but couldn't see anyone and when he spun back around there was a woman sitting on the stool next to him, taking off her coat and scarf.

'Hi.' Ryan said in a slightly sarcastic voice.

'Hi,' was the reply.

'Anything I can help you with, or am I supposed to know you?'

'Yes and no,' she said with a smile in return.

After a minute in silence, she began.

'My name is Jane Campbell and I work in the drugs enforcement division of Interpol, and I have just witnessed you running into central station chasing a man who was at a meeting with someone we have a very keen interest in.'

She said it with authority and conviction, Ryan thought. But not to offend.

'Ok.' said Ryan.

'So, our thinking is, that you were either returning a lost wallet or you were trying to speak with him, the latter being my guess.'

She was around 5ft 9 with blonde hair that was shoulder length, she was wearing fitted trousers with a different colour blazer and a white blouse underneath, Ryan would have guessed she was about thirty-seven years old and looked good for it, really good. She also seemed to omit a confidence that didn't come across as arrogant and she intrigued him straight away.

'I would class myself as being someone who can read people pretty well, but I'm afraid I will need to see some id.' Replied Ryan.

'I hoped you would say that.'

She reached into her back pocket and brought out a leather wallet and passed it to him. He opened it and saw a picture of the woman sitting next to him, the photo was maybe two years old, but she looked similar to how she looked now.

'So why would Interpol be on the hunt for such a guy?'

'I'm not sure I want to put my cards on the table just yet. Why were you chasing after him?'

'I'm not much of a card player myself.' Ryan replied with a smirk.

'You mind if I have a beer with you?'

'Sure, don't see why not.'

***

After half an hour of small talk and two more beers each, they agreed that they both hadn't eaten all day and decided on getting some food. They left the bar and headed into the city Centre to find some dinner.

Ryan knew after about ten minutes of the small talk he liked Jane and felt reasonably sure he could trust her, obviously not with any details, but he didn't need to be so cautious.

They found a Chinese restaurant after a short walk and got a table for two at the window, they ordered a starting platter for two and two diet Pepsi's.

'So, if we both trust that we are working towards the same thing here, I am more than happy to share the little details that I do actually know, if you are that is?' Ryan said.

'I believe I can do that.' Jane replied still looking down at her food.

Ryan took a sip of his drink and began.

'I was told to be at a meeting point near a café that was situated at the entrance to Dam Square, I won't reveal the exact location for now, but I had to be there for a specific time and try to gather as much information as I could. Unfortunately, all I really managed to gather was what appeared to be a meeting between three men of varied ages, which at first seemed civilised but then quickly grew from a scuffle, to what I assume ended with a kidnapping.'

'Sounds about right,' said Jane.

Jane was clearly going through in her mind what she knew, what she could tell, and what she wanted to tell.

'Feel free to jump in anytime soon, I'm running out of cards over here.'

Jane smiled, just a little.

'The man at the meeting with the mustache is a Dutch national who Interpol have knowledge off and an interest in, he is known as Mr. king, I won't go into every detail, but he is a major drug dealer in Amsterdam city Centre and the surrounding areas.'

Ryan kept her gaze but didn't speak, prompting her to continue.

'As far as exporting goes, we're not sure, but the turnaround and street value of cocaine he sells alone as well as heroin and meth, are as much as we know of in Holland. We have been tracking him alongside the Dutch intelligence services for just over a year and are close to having all we need to make an arrest.'

'A year?' asked Ryan, surprised.

'When you go after a guy like this you have to be sure that what you have is going to stick, because if it doesn't, he will go to ground and that will be that.'

'Well, I have learned a hundred times more in five minutes talking with you, than I did at the café.'

'So, what was your next move going to be — if I hadn't followed you here?' She asked.

Ryan looked up and squinted his eyes.

Jane laughed and sipped her Pepsi.

'I'm making contact with one of my team tomorrow to de-brief and hopefully find out more,' he continued, 'do you have any information on the man I chased into central station?'

'You weren't the only one who chased him in there. I had an agent sitting at a bar three streets down and when he saw him running, he followed him also.'

'I never saw anyone else running,'

'He was behind you.'

Ryan tried to recall someone moving fast behind him but couldn't remember.

'To be honest, we have never come across the man before, seemed to be a bit out of place we thought.'

'Yeah, that's the impression I got too,' Ryan said, then continued, 'I don't really know who he was with at the meeting either or if he was a third party.'

'The one good thing about my guy which should help us both was, he managed to get on the train.'

They sat silently for a few seconds. Ryan wondered how her agent managed to catch the train when he was behind him, and he didn't.

'Have you heard from him yet?' Ryan said a little too eagerly.

'Ten minutes ago, he was one carriage in front of him and is planning on following him. I have told him to keep his distance and let me know as soon as possible if he gets any information.'

Ryan took a bite of a spring roll and took his time chewing it, he was going through what he knew again and was trying to make something of what he had just learnt.

They were just finishing up and Ryan paid the bill, they agreed to meet tomorrow afternoon to go over what they had found out, if anything, but in the meantime, they exchanged numbers and told each other if anything came up before tomorrow they would be in touch.

They headed out of the restaurant and walked down the side of the canal and towards the Damrak, the city was now buzzing with people, they stopped outside central station and stood awkwardly for a minute.

Jane then began, 'I wasn't sure about telling you this because I'm not a hundred percent sure myself.'

Ryan perked up.

'The man at the meeting, with the jet-black hair who got dragged away, I'm guessing you noticed him?' She said sarcastically.

'Yes,' Ryan replied.

'If he is who I think he is and my agent who was on the street thinks the same, then he is one of the biggest drug dealers in central Europe and has only been seen in public twice in the last five years.'

Ryan left Jane and headed to his hotel bar for a bourbon, or two.

Chapter 12

Ryan ate his poached egg and toast in a café a short walk from his hotel, he also made sure his tea was poured in front of him this time.

The city seemed brighter this morning, the sky was clear, and the temperature seemed to be that bit colder. Winter was already here but the snow had still only threatened.

Ryan had been up early and spent 45 minutes in the hotel gym, working out and thinking. He knew before he left yesterday morning that his old unit would be involved in this somehow and he was now sure of it.

He found himself starting to go over the meeting in the café, like a play he was writing in his head.

Why meet in a public place that was so central, was his main thought, and what could they have been there to discuss. And was coming back with the slim man after leaving, intentional, or was it just coincidental. Most of all, he thought, what could have been said to get the reaction it did.

He knew that to keep going over it wasn't going to help. Once he had spoken to his boss, he could start making plans and put things into action.

He hadn't heard from Jane since he had left her the day before, but they had arranged to meet at four o'clock at a vendor that sat in front of the canal next to the station. So, with a few hours to spare he had decided to make a visit to the café where the meeting was yesterday, and hopefully pick up any information that might help.

As he approached the café, he could see it was open for business. There was a police patrol car sitting outside though, so Ryan walked across the square to the other side of the road from where the car was sitting and went in. He ordered a caramel latte and sat as close to where

Mr. king had sat yesterday. He leaned over and looked up at the hotel that he had been watching from and found what he thought was his room.

The waitress arrived shortly after with his coffee and he asked in a manner that seemed more conversational, than interrogation.

'That was some ordeal in here yesterday, was it not?'

'Yeah, it was,' she replied.

'Was everyone ok?' Ryan asked.

'Yeah, no one was hurt, I was on my break in the back but heard it all.'

'Did you see anything that you thought was strange apart from the obvious?'

'Are you with the police?' she asked.

Ryan knew he had gone too far.

'No, it was just that I saw it all on TV and thought it must have been terrifying to have witnessed it.'

The waitress opened her mouth as if she was going to say something but then gave a smile and returned to the counter.

Ryan finished his drink, stood, wrapped himself up and headed back out onto the street.

The police car was still sitting where it was earlier and the two guys inside were still staring out the front window in deep conversation. Ryan started to make his way toward the station to catch the train for the stadium, he wanted to be there early enough to wander around and get his bearings.

He had just passed the café window when, from an alley that the man he'd chased yesterday came from, the waitress appeared and grabbed his arm — she was clearly on a break now as she had a half-smoked cigarette in her hand.

'I wasn't sure if there was anything in this yesterday, but when you asked about anything strange happening it made me think.'

Ryan had a look around to see if anyone was paying them any attention.

'When I was on break, I was sitting in the back on my phone when a young slim man in a suit appeared from the side entrance, everyone just looked at him as he entered and he quite casually told everyone not to panic and if there was any commotion he was from the police and he would deal with it.'

It had to be the man that Ryan had chased into the station.

'Can you tell me anymore about this man?'

'The only thing that stood out was that he was very young looking and had a strong English accent, but that isn't that strange.'

Ryan thanked her and headed for the stadium.

Chapter 13

Ryan was back on the same platform that he had stood on a day earlier. He could still see that smug face staring out at him as the train was sucked into the tunnel.

The train he was now waiting on approached and he boarded. He clumsily stumbled his way to the last carriage as the train departed and threw him in all directions. He steadied himself before standing at the same window as the man from yesterday had, just as the train picked up speed and disappeared into the tunnel, again.

There were two stops before Ryan's, the station he was getting off at was called *The Stadium*, coincidently. He was feeling a little excited at the thought of going to a football match, something he hadn't done that many times before and especially as it was to be at the famous Ajax football club.

He checked his watch as the train started to slow, 11:35, he would have plenty of time and planned to take a long walk around the stadium. He looked at his ticket again and found the gate and seat number, f side – row 34 – seat 4.

He put the ticket in his inside jacket pocket and headed for the door. He stepped out onto the platform and looked up at what was the most spectacular looking station he had seen; it was like a huge glass bubble that covered the whole of the station and continued onto the escalators that led down to the stadium itself. He slipped in behind a large group of young fans and made his way down. As he stepped off the escalator and came out from under the bubble, he was standing twenty feet from the stadium building, he felt dwarfed as he looked up at it, it seemed to take up the whole sky. He stopped and stared for a moment before making his way around to the north end.

The atmosphere was electric, there were thousands of people, mostly draped in red and white, the team colours. Some we're walking round, some talking, some singing but the majority were standing at the many bars drinking. Ryan spent the next half hour taking it all in as he wandered aimlessly through the crowds. He made sure he found his gate that he would use to get into the stadium even though he planned on waiting till the game had kicked off before taking to his seat, he would be able to check who was around him or if he could notice his contact first.

He checked his watch again, 12:20, ten minutes to go, and as if all at once the outside of the stadium vanished, like a mass exodus, they were all hurrying to get inside for the kickoff.

Again, the sense of excitement from the fans was overwhelming, the anticipation was building all the time. Sporadic outbursts of singing would start up from one corner and be quickly picked up and ring round the large groups of supporters.

Ryan approached his gate just as the last few stragglers were rushing by and passed through the security turnstile, he got his ticket stub back and headed up the stairs.

The main walkway, where all the food stands, and toilets were, was still busy with fans getting last minute snacks and beers. Ryan waited until it cleared out a bit before he climbed the last few steps up and onto the terrace — where he was met with a wall of noise. He was amazed by the scene in front of him, the stadium was packed, and the roar was deafening as the players got ready for kick off.

After watching the game for a few minutes, Ryan noticed the man he was meeting as he walked along the terrace behind the row his seat was in. From what he could make out of his contact, he thought he could see a slight resemblance between them, which he found strange.

He was sitting in what would have been seat 3. Ryan walked down a few steps and then excused himself as he squeezed past a man and a woman who were sitting in the first two seats, then his contact and he sat in seat number four. He sat in silence and watched the game for nearly ten minutes before any of them spoke.

'I'm seriously hoping you have some good news for me.' The contact said with no emotion.

Ryan turned in his seat and blew out his cheeks, that, was not what he wanted to hear.

'I was hoping to get some good news from you to be honest, I'm still in the dark about this whole thing.'

'What did you gather from the meeting yesterday?'

Ryan took a few seconds before answering.

'What I gathered from the whole thing is that no one seems to have any clue what the hell was going on.'

The contact looked at the ground impatiently.

'This whole operation is a mess, from what I can figure,' the contact said, eventually.

Ryan knew that anyway.

'My name is Michael by the way,' he reached out and shook his hand, Ryan did the same.

'Before we go any further, I'm what you would most likely call the number two of our agency. My official title is assistant director, and I was spending the weekend in Barcelona when I got a call first thing this morning, I was told to make my way to this stadium to meet with you.'

He continued. 'The head of our agency, we believe, was working this case himself, and at approximately 9:55 a.m. yesterday morning he went completely off grid, no contact from him, no mobile phone signal nothing and it has thrown headquarters into meltdown.'

Ryan listened closely.

'What I have been brought up to speed on so far is that at the last minute you were specifically assigned this case, which I believe was passed on to you by Jones, is that correct?'

Ryan nodded and thought about those BMW heated seats as he sat there frozen.

'What I found out since, is that we received intelligence from a reliable source that a person of interest to us was meeting with a small-time drug dealer in the Centre of Amsterdam yesterday morning. The man we believed was going to be there, is a major drug dealer that goes by the name of Sonny, and if this turns out to be correct, then it is the first time he has been seen in public in almost eighteen months and would be completely out of character for him.'

Ryan thought about Jane but decided to keep her role quiet for now.

'Do we have any images or a way of identifying him?' Ryan said.

'To be honest the last picture we have goes back six years. What we do know, is that he is about 5ft 10, maybe in his early fifties and has jet black hair.'

Ryan turned around and looked straight at him for the first time. He thought that they both looked similar up close also, similar features.

'Everything that you have said is obviously information I was not privy too, but what I can tell you is the man you just described fits my description of the man that our old friends pulled out of that café yesterday morning.'

'And can you be sure?' Michael replied.

'Given the description you have just gave me I would

be 95 percent sure.'

'How do you know it is our old friends?'

'Knowledge of how they operate. They certainly had their team on the ground when I arrived, one calling it and at least one muscle that I could see, more than likely there would have been someone in the café too.'

'Ok,' Michael replied.

Ryan continued. 'Also, the team that came in the car to extract him was flown in that morning the way they usually do it, I was on the same plane as them yesterday.'

'Now were getting somewhere,' Michael replied.

He continued. 'I'm assuming that you got the number plate, but I doubt it will come back with anything.'

'Correct,' said Ryan 'I checked it last night, it came back as stolen,'

'Is there anything else that you can think of that could be a source or a lead?'

Ryan then began to tell the story of the slim man in the suit. He told him about the chase and the train he left on and that he felt the man was very important to the whole thing, which Michael agreed with and said he would take it to the team and try to identify or find more details on.

'What is my next move?' Ryan asked.

'Comb the café again and try to speak to anyone that may be familiar with these men, small time dealers, but as always stay under the radar until I hear back on the slim guy. We will contact you on your mobile if there is any news, stay in touch and stay alert, if anyone knows we're on this they might have eyes on you, especially if your right and our old friends are at the party.'

Michael stood up and stared at the field for a second. 'Good work yesterday' he said finally and left Ryan sitting. He squeezed past the people in seat one and two and headed out of the stadium.

Ryan sat for a bit longer, thinking about what they had

spoken about. He came here looking for a bit of clarity, but it turned out he knew more than anyone else did, according to Michael at least.

The referee blew his whistle to signal the end of the half, Ryan took this opportunity to blend in with what appeared to be half the stadium, as they got up and headed for refreshments.

He looked out at the car park and surrounding areas of the stadium as he rode down the escalator, the place was deserted. He looped round the back of the arena as he left, just to see it more than anything else. He still couldn't believe the size and grandeur of it.

He walked up the stairs to the station platform, the train was sitting waiting as he got there. He stepped on and found a seat near the back.

***

The man at the stadium watched as Ryan climbed onto the train before phoning his boss.

The slim guy answered his phone on the first ring. 'They have just made contact in the stadium; I couldn't get close enough to hear anything, but they spoke for nearly fifteen minutes.'

'Who did he meet with?' the slim guy asked.

'Their number two, Michael is his name, the one we couldn't get to.'

'Anything else? Are you still following him now?'

'No, I lost him when he caught the train back to the city Centre.'

The slim guy hung up the phone.

Chapter 14

Jane was seriously thinking about going into the shop across the street from the vender, where she had been standing for nearly twenty minutes waiting on Ryan, to buy herself a thicker jacket. She had never felt this cold in all the time she had spent in Amsterdam.

Her day had been pretty mundane so far, even though everything was in motion she found herself waiting on other people to get in touch to begin to piece this together. She had managed to speak to her agent — Klass — on the phone while she ate lunch in her hotel. He had followed the man from the café as far as a town just outside of Dortmund, four stops from the city's central station, a town called Bochum. Klass had followed him from the train and about half a mile into the town Centre, before a black BMW X6 pulled over to the side of the road and picked him up. At that point Klass made his way back to the train station to see if he could get a picture of him from the station's CCTV, which he did after an hour and a half of trying. The picture was from just over 60 yards away and was quite blurry, but he knew his tech guys would be able to enhance it, you could still make out who it was though. He then checked into a small hotel and went over everything before contacting Jane.

***

Since leaving the stadium and exiting central station Ryan had circled around the canal and the Damrak a few times, just in case he had someone following him, which he began to feel was maybe the case. He spotted Jane at the vendor at 3:45 p.m. — on time and shivering by the looks of her. She was dressed as smart as she had been yesterday, different colour of fitted jeans with a neck scarf and warmer jacket on this time. She smiled at him as he approached and as he got close was about to lean in to greet him, but rather awkwardly put her hands in her pockets and smiled instead.

'Coffee?' Ryan opened with before Jane had the chance to speak.

She nodded and turned and walked to the nearest bridge to cross over the canal.

They found a café and ordered two flat whites and a sandwich each.

Jane began to fill Ryan in about what her man had reported to her that morning, Ryan had told her what had been said at his meeting, not that there was much to say, but he told her anyway. They sat and discussed what was the best way to move forward.

'I have run it by my boss that I will be working closely with you regarding this case, and I know he will run some background checks on you, are you ok with this?' Jane asked.

'Sure, I was expecting you would have, and I knew someone higher up would have a look at me, I'm sure they will do the same at my end when I tell them about you, but I think I trust you regardless.'

Jane smiled for the second time since meeting him today. They finished their coffee and ate their sandwiches while staring out the window.

***

The man with the jet-black hair was called Sonny, not his birth name, but that was what he was known by these days, and he was getting restless. He had been stuck in the hold room in the unit's temporary base for not even a day and was not handling it very well. He knew he still had another 24 hours to wait but he wanted things to begin right now. The guys who had him captured were competent, he knew that but at the same time knew he could handle them all on his own, no bother.

For the brief minutes he had spoken to his contact before he was wrestled out of the café in Dam square, he knew that their target had been captured at a similar time as he was and that he was currently being held somewhere in Germany. He had also been told that they had been able to identify who the man was that had been flipped from the unit that was holding him, he had tried to work it out, but no one had given anything away, as of yet. He checked his watch again and let out a sigh, he just hoped that his man was doing all he could and was capable of pulling this off.

Chapter 15

'How much information do you think we can get from locals around here?' Ryan asked Jane.

'I know of a few guys but only through reports or the odd time I have been part of interviewing if they have been brought in for questioning.' Jane replied. 'Klass was always the one who worked the streets and knew most of the small-time dealers and crooks,' she paused while thinking. 'Although there was this one informant. I dealt with him a few years ago, he helped us out with a case and every now and then he pops up with some good information. I will get his number from Klass and see where he is these days.'

They made their way back towards Dam square and headed north, nearer to the outskirts of the city. They hoped to find someone that might talk while they waited to hear back from Klass.

'I think we need to be pretty clever here, if we find someone who looks like they might be dealing, we start up a conversation and see what we can get from him.'

'I think we play it cool and see what we get from Klass' man first, if we start snooping around just now and someone gets wind of this then we could scare everyone from talking.'

They walked aimlessly through the streets. Ryan was starting to think that all this waiting was slowing things down when he needed to be getting things moving.

He was about to suggest splitting up and going their own way for a bit when Jane's mobile started ringing, they both stopped as she answered it.

Klass had spoken to the man less than three months ago and he came up with some good stuff that had really helped him, but this time he seemed a bit more reluctant to meet. Klass had explained it was with his boss and her understudy, which Ryan found funny. The contact had said he would be in Rembrandt Park in half an hour and would meet only if he thought the coast was clear.

***

The slim guy answered on the third ring and was sounding impatient.

'What.'

'The guy we flipped who is watching Sonny says we need to start soon, or they are going to move him again.' The slim guy was quiet.

'Tell him we need another 24 hours at least.' He finally said.

'I have.'

'What have we got on him?' The slim guy replied.

'His wife and dog.'

'Is he scared?'

'Absolutely.'

'Tell him we have to wait to sort out logistics and we will go as soon as we can, but we need the 24 hours or else he knows how these things go. I also need you to get out here, tell your bosses whatever you want but you need to get here as soon as possible. You will be picked up from the Euro tunnel and can make your way to Dortmund with one of our men.'

He paused waiting for a reply.

'Hurry up and get here and phone me when you are.' The slim guy hung up the phone.

Chapter 16

Klass' contact of sorts was called Alex, and he was already sitting on a bench near the entrance of the park when Ryan and Jane arrived. He was in his late twenties with scruffy hair and a beard, he was underdressed for the weather and came across a little agitated. His left hand was shaking as if he was on drugs, needed drugs, or had drugs and was desperate to take them. Ryan and Jane approached; he nodded as he looked up at them with sunken eyes.

'Alex.' Ryan said as he sat next to him.

Jane sat on the other side.

They were all looking out at the park, the sun was bright but starting to go down. The trees were empty of leaves and the park was empty of people, they sat for a minute before Alex began.

'I think I know what you're going to ask, and I will just tell you what I know and then I'm going to leave.'

He spoke fast but clearly.

'About three weeks ago things started to change around here, there has always been a kind of hierarchy in all this madness you know. The small guys knew who the middle guys were, and the middle guys knew who the big guys were, and everyone knew who the bosses were, and then slowly things started to change. We heard that one of the big guys, probably the biggest, had started to wrap things up, paid everyone out, didn't even collect all his debt, just took what he could and set everyone free you know…'

Ryan could see Alex relax a bit, his leg wasn't shaking as much, and he sat back on the bench. He seemed pretty smart and Ryan kind of liked him, for some strange reason.

Alex continued. 'So, as you can imagine all the small

guys are telling the middle guys to piss off and the middle guys likewise. So now you got everyone kind of meeting in the middle and trying to claim certain areas for themselves. Shit thing for us at the bottom of the pile is that the drugs are up two euros, because the bosses ain't bringing it in anymore, so the demand isn't going to be met so the product gets pricier, which sucks you know. I'm telling you things are only going to get worse before it levels out. My usual dealer has just sold me his last bag and says he isn't sure what he is going to do now, maybe he could get a job.'

Alex laughed to himself before breaking into a coughing fit, Ryan caught Jane's eye and made an expression as if to say, we don't really need to say anything here.

Once Alex composed himself, he started up again.

'I don't know if this is what you guys want to hear but it's all I got. I'm not even sure if this is true to be honest, but I do know that something is going down you know. I heard most of this from my dealer, he says that there has been a guy kicking about here recently too, most of it has come from him, he is the one who is paying them off and telling them how it's to be now.'

'You have a name?' Ryan asked.

'Sure,' Alex said.

Ryan looked at Jane and smirked.

'Fancy telling us?'

'From what I hear his name is Clarke, posh name I think, you know.'

Ryan tried to remember the name from somewhere in the last 48 hours, but he couldn't place it.

'If everyone came together and worked as a team, I think the whole thing could be better you know.'

He was beginning to wander now. Ryan thought.

Ryan asked, 'Could you recognise this Clarke if you

saw him again?'

'No, I haven't seen him, only been told things from my dealer.'

'Like what?'

'Says he seems clever, but that might not mean much because my dealer is dumb as shit, he doesn't think he has much to do with drugs himself, more of a businessman.'

'Do you have a description?'

Alex stood up. 'Yeah man, real skinny, dresses smart and talks like he's from England or somewhere.'

Ryan stood up next to him and handed him a 100 Euro note. 'Get yourself to a restaurant and get some food then find a cough bottle and a winter jacket.'

'With a hundred Euro?' Alex smirked. 'Are you high?'

Ryan laughed.

Alex hurried off out the park and across the canal and disappeared into the shadows. Ryan sat down again and slid up next to Jane, she was on her phone typing, he let her finish. She looked up from the phone and turned to Ryan as the sun was about to disappear from the horizon and said to him… 'so the slim guy is called Clarke then.'

Sonny was climbing the walls and didn't think he could wait any longer. He hated the thought that there were things going on outside these four walls that he had planned for months and put into action, but couldn't see happening. He knew actions had been taken by now and hoped he would get out of here soon, but he was really starting to struggle. His door opened and one of the men came in with a takeaway bag of food, this was another part of it he hated, eating like a dog. He grabbed the bag and stared at the man who had delivered it. He thought about smashing the man in the head and grabbing his gun when the man took a step closer and lowered his head and said.

'Be patient, this time tomorrow we will be ready to move.'

The man left and shut the door. Sonny smiled, he thought to himself that he was the last one he thought would have been flipped. He opened the bag and took out his burger and ate it with a smile.

***

Jane was forwarding the name Alex gave them onto Klass who was in Dortmund. Ryan thought he should call it in as well, see if his team could help come up with any leads too. They had got up from the park bench and were heading back towards the river. Ryan wasn't really one for texting, so he took his mobile that he got from the locker at Edinburgh airport and tried to call Michael, it went straight to voicemail, so he phoned head office instead. It was answered by one of the girls at the front desk.

'Good afternoon, Paper Street Logistics,'

'Hi, it's Ryan 0412, calling for the finance manager please?' They all had specific reference numbers and depending what manager they asked for it would be put through to the correct department.

'Just a second, Sir.'

The phone started to play what would be described as a copy of a Coldplay song, he listened to it for a few seconds before it was answered.

An eager sounding man answered and asked for the bank account number, another code to confirm the agent's identity. Ryan gave the code and was told he was speaking to Jones who asked how he could help.

Ryan knew who it was the second Jones answered.

'Jones, I'm still on business in Amsterdam and I need you to check a name for me that has just come up. We believe it to be a person of interest and need you to find out what you can on him.'

Jones sat up straight and grabbed a pen.

'We believe him to be of a slim build and around six feet tall, he seems to be some kind of businessman with possibly an English accent. He has been in Amsterdam city Centre recently and we believe him to have travelled by train in the direction of Dortmund in the last 24 hours.'

Jones started to tense his back, no way, not this quick.

Ryan continued 'we reckon him to be in his mid-thirties also, unfortunately we don't have a last name but we're sure his first name to be Clarke.'

Jones froze as a bead of sweat trickled down the side of his head onto the paper he was writing on.

'Ok Ryan, we will check this out and be in touch as soon as possible.' He tried not to sound as terrified as he felt when he said it.

***

Jones stood up from his desk and picked up his jacket from the back of his chair. He said to his boss he was taking his lunch early today and made his way through the office to the front door, he could feel his hand shaking in his pocket. He headed out the front of the building and onto the street. He lit a cigarette as soon as he got out, it didn't help with his shaking hands. Instead of going into his local café he just kept walking, he needed to think, he needed time to come up with some way of getting out of this shit he had found himself in. He took out his mobile phone as he stood leaning on the railing that surrounded Westminster Abbey. He looked up at the Houses of Parliament and Big Ben, which was hiding behind a cloak of scaffolding, shit, shit, shit, he thought to himself. He put his password in, and his phone came to life, he dialed the only number that he had saved in his contacts list, he didn't get an answer.

Chapter 18

Ryan and Jane had left the park and were now back in the city Centre. It was beginning to get dark, and they walked quickly as the temperature was starting to fall fast; until any intel got back to them, they didn't know which way to turn next.

'Klass says that this information could come in handy.' Jane said. 'He has two local agents out making enquiries just now and will pass the name onto them, meanwhile he is holed up in one of our safe houses trying to get hold of any records we might have, to try and pick our man out. Did you get anything at your end?'

'No.' Ryan said, 'They took all the details and will run it through our records and see if anything comes up, they will be in contact.'

They kept walking in silence for a bit.

'I think we need to look at this from another angle.' Ryan said. 'I'm struggling to put this Clarke into the picture. If he is trying to help one side or the other then why would he turn up at the café late, he should have been there from the start, or have just stayed away altogether. I can't think why he would appear in the middle of the meeting and cause the commotion that he did.'

Jane thought about this for a bit.

'I never really thought about that, it's like he had a message to pass on, or information to give one of them maybe.'

They continued walking for another fifteen minutes, talking about the different theories that could explain it. Ryan had unconsciously started heading in the direction of his hotel and they had ended up a street away from its entrance before he realised.

'Isn't this where you're staying?' Jane said.

'It is, I wasn't even thinking where we were heading.'

They looked at each other awkwardly. Ryan then said, 'If you haven't got any plans, I was going to get a quick change then head for some dinner, if you want to come up you can, or maybe meet me later at a restaurant.'

Jane blushed slightly, then said, 'I wasn't planning on getting changed again, so I can come and wait if you won't be long.'

'Five minutes tops.' Ryan smiled.

They took the stairs to the top floor; Ryan led the way. He was going to ask her about where she fancied eating but left it and got out his key card as he approached his room. He unlocked the door and held it open as she walked through. The room was much nicer than any she had stayed in when she got moved to the city.

'There is a bar over by the fridge if you fancy a beer, I just have to change my shirt and jacket.' he said as he stepped into the bathroom.

Jane took off her jacket and sat it on the bed as she walked over to the bar. She took out two beers and opened them.

'Won't you get charged for these?' she shouted through the half open door.

'No, it's fine, it's all free.' he shouted back.

She sat on the bed as Ryan came out of the bathroom and took his beer from the dresser. He had changed his shirt and washed his face but left a few of the buttons undone — his shirt hanging out of his trousers. He sat on the chair.

He looked at Jane sitting perched on the end of the bed, she looked amazing and very relaxed, he felt weird about asking her up and didn't think she would have, but was glad she did.

'What you got in mind for eating tonight?' Ryan said.

'Not sure,' she replied.

'I don't like the thought of walking about the streets in the cold again,' he said.

'We could eat in the hotel then, maybe, is it any good?'

'Pretty good,' Ryan said as he stood up and headed over towards the bed and picked up the hotel menu as he did. He sat on the bed and passed it to her.

She moved up a little so they both could read it, he placed his hand down next to her and turned to look at her, she held her gaze on the menu for a second before looking up. 'I'm not that hungry to be honest.' said Jane quietly.

'I can wait.' Ryan replied smiling.

They both leaned in closer. Ryan's hand now on top of Jane's as he got close enough to kiss her, Jane moved in and closed her eyes, she was waiting to feel his lips on hers. Just before she did, her mobile phone began to ring.

They both stopped and looked at the phone ringing on the bed behind them, the screen was lit up and flashing with the name Klass on it. They looked at each other again and smiled in frustration.

She answered as she stood up and walked over to the window to get a better reception.

She was on the phone for no more than two minutes and had only said three words, the last word she said was *shit* and hung up. She turned and looked at Ryan.

'What is it?' he asked concerned.

'One of Klass' men has just been shot and killed in a bar in Dortmund, he had phoned Klass ten minutes before saying he was following a strong lead.'

***

Jones never got an answer, so he headed back to his desk and asked to speak to his boss when he had a second. He typed up the report of what he had wrote down during the call he received from Ryan and lifted a copy of the file. He explained that he had helped as much as he could from his desk but felt he would now be of more use if he headed out, and assisted the team in Amsterdam, His boss went through all the information they had and read the report again and agreed, reluctantly. He understood that he would be more help to them if he was in the field.

Jones grabbed all he needed from his desk and took his overnight bag from his locker, he logged onto the company's system to update his status to 'in the field' then left the office building and headed for the underground. He had got one of the office workers to book him a seat on the Eurostar for later that night.

He got out of the underground and caught the train to Dover; it would take 50 minutes and would give him the chance to look over some paperwork. But first he had to try Clarke again. He took out his phone and dialed again, this time it was answered on the first ring.

'They got your name.' Jones said with little emotion.

There was no reply, the phone hung up.

Chapter 19

Clarke couldn't talk, he had just been informed that one of his men had gotten into an altercation with someone that was snooping around one of their pubs asking questions, luckily it wasn't the one in particular, but it was still going to bring some heat onto him.

'Tell me what happened?' He said in a quiet voice.

'He told me a man came into the bar asking if anyone knew of an English man called Clarke who might have been hanging around the city recently; he said he might have links with several nightclubs in the area.'

Clarke was listening.

'He was told no, but he was pushy, he was asked to leave but got aggressive and noticed one of our men who had grabbed him had a gun, so he had pulled his.'

'Then what?' Asked Clarke.

'They managed to get him out the back door into the alley, but our man got spooked and shot him in the chest, the guy was dead instantly.'

'Couldn't you cover it up?'

'No chance, the whole pub heard, the place was packed.'

'Ok, does the shooter know the deal?'

'Yeah, he does now, he will say it was all him but the police where all over the club within ten minutes.'

'It will be fine.' Clarke said sternly.

'Give them what they need and let them get on with it, I can't have them looking into anymore of our clubs.'

He had to get the wheels rolling on this and get the plan into action, he didn't want things getting jeopardised before they had even begun.

Chapter 20

Ryan stood up, buttoned his shirt, and tucked it in his trousers, now he had a problem. It was fine that he was working with Jane in Amsterdam and that they could help each other out, but this wasn't one of his team that had been killed in Dortmund. He also knew at the same time it could maybe lead him to Clarke. He picked up his cell and tried Michael, his number two again, but it went straight to voicemail.

'Any luck?' Jane asked.

'No, voicemail again,' he replied.

'I have to get to Dortmund.'

'I know, I think I do too, but I will need to run it past my boss, and I can't get hold of him.'

He stood at the window thinking as Jane put her jacket on behind him.

'Can you get us two tickets on a train tonight?' Ryan asked.

Jane took out her phone and began tapping away on it, after a few minutes, she said.

'We have two seats booked for the 7:20 p.m. express train to Dortmund, we need to be at central station one hour before.'

Ryan picked up his jacket and put it on, he looked at Jane and smiled, she smiled back.

'We will have time to grab some dinner before we head to the station.'

She nodded as they left the room and down the stairs.

***

Jones was in the departure lounge of the Eurostar station waiting on the train to be boarded. He had written an email to Clarke explaining that he was on his way to

Calais and would be at the meeting point early tomorrow morning to meet the driver, he hadn't gotten a reply, as of yet. He took out his works cell phone and dialed a number not saved in it, but which was written in the file.

***

Ryan and Jane were sitting in a pub just off the north of the Damrak and had both ordered a burger and a Pepsi. They were just finishing and getting ready to pay the bill when Ryan's phone began ringing, he hoped it was Michael calling him back as he went into his pocket and took out the phone, he saw it was someone from head office.

'Ryan speaking,' he said.

'Ryan it's Jones, we have looked into your client and can't come up with any significant information on him, without a surname, he is hard to find.'

Ryan looked annoyed.

'What I might add though, is that I will be coming out to assist you with any help you might need in finding more about this client.'

Ryan still didn't speak.

'I'm boarding the Eurostar in a few hours and should be in Amsterdam about midday tomorrow.'

'Ok.' Ryan replied, slightly confused.

Chapter 21

They collected their tickets from the station kiosk; the train was departing in ten minutes. It was a nonstop journey straight to central station in Dortmund, it would take two hours and thirty-five minutes. Ryan hoped to have a look around when they got there but knew it would be late, if they managed to catch up with Klass and get filled in on any details about what happened to his agent being killed, he could then make his own enquiries in the morning.

The train journey seemed to go by pretty quick, Ryan and Jane didn't really talk about work, they seemed to talk more about themselves and their lives rather than the case, Ryan thought it might have been awkward after what had happened in his hotel room, or what was about to happen, but Jane seemed to have forgotten about it for now and Ryan was happy enough with that.

***

Michael was starting to get a bad feeling. Apart from the fact that his boss had now been missing with absolutely no contact for 36 hours, he couldn't get a hold of Ryan, and head office hadn't come up with any information on the man that Ryan had given them the details of. He was still in Amsterdam and needed to make a move, he had to get a hold of Ryan and come up with a plan.

***

The train pulled into the station and Ryan and Jane both got to their feet, put on their jackets and grabbed their bags. Jane had spoken for ten minutes to Klass, who had arranged a lift for them at Dortmund station to bring them to the safe house, where they would be filled in on the shooting at the nightclub.

Dortmund city Centre wasn't quite as cold as Amsterdam, but it was trying its best. They walked through the station easily enough as it was quiet, due to the time of night, it was mostly the people from the train that had just arrived and a few groups of people hanging about, talking, and waiting for their trains, or saying goodbye to friends who were about to leave. There were also a few cleaners pushing bin carts around picking up litter.

They came out the sliding doors and saw a car waiting at the side of the road with the driver leaning against the passenger door smoking a cigarette, he saw them and threw it on the ground and stamped on it before taking Jane's bag. Ryan walked round the car so he would be sitting in the seat directly behind the driver. He looked at the clock before he got in, 10:19 p.m. the temperature read minus 1 underneath.

***

Clarke received the email from Jones and replied when he got the chance. He told him that one of his men, the same one who had followed Ryan to the stadium, was already taking care of the customs officer and would pick him up from the Eurostar station afterwards. He would then take him into Amsterdam and give him further instructions. Jones opened up the email and read it once, deleted it and closed over his laptop.

***

The car Ryan and Jane were traveling in was a VW Tiguan, it was a comfortable 4x4. Ryan was remembering the route from the train station to the safe house — just in case he needed to make the journey himself.

The driver's name was Gregor, and he wasn't very talkative, he said that he knew the agent who had been killed and had worked with him for many years and never really spoke after that. After fifteen minutes of winding through city streets and one-way roads they pulled into a complex that looked like it should have been in Monte Carlo. When Ryan had heard they were heading to an Interpol safe house, he had imagined a rundown flat above a shop, but this was a high-end luxury apartment, the car park had a security gate and the building itself looked very expensive.

They got out of the car and headed to the building entrance. Gregor held up a key fob and was beeped into the main foyer. It was tiled with marble that was so clean, you could eat your dinner off it. Ryan looked at Jane as they approached the lift, but she must have been used to this type of building. The door opened and they went in. Gregor pressed for the fifth floor and the elevator kicked into action. They got out as the lift doors opened, they turned left and walked to the end of the corridor, they stopped at room 43. After knocking twice, the door was opened by who he presumed was Klass.

It wasn't, it turned out to be another agent called Jari. Klass was sitting at a breakfast bar in the corner surrounded by computers and pieces of paper.

'Hey, how you doing?' Jane asked.

'It was a bit of a shock; rest of the guys are angry.' Klass replied.

'We will get them.' Jane said, unsure. 'This is Ryan, the guy I told you I have been working with.'

Ryan walked over and shook his hand, 'pleased to meet you Klass.'

'You too, Ryan, can we get down to business?' Klass

said sitting back on his stool.

He wasn't what Ryan had imagined when Jane had spoken about him. He was maybe in his early forties, not quite as lean as himself but well kept, he was wearing grey chinos with casual navy shoes and a navy polo shirt, he was maybe six feet tall with a shaved head and beard, he looked very focused and very sure of himself.

Gregor made everyone a coffee and they all sat at the breakfast bar as Klass filled them in on the events of the last 18 hours.

'When I got off the train from Amsterdam, I followed who I now know is Clarke for about half a mile. I tried to get pictures of him on my phone, but I couldn't get a clear shot of his face, I left the station and headed east towards the city Centre. I stayed well back from him and tried not to get spotted, he walked for about a mile before crossing the road. I tried to keep up but as soon as he got on the other side of the road a car pulled up and he got in before speeding away.'

'Did you get the license number?' Jane asked.

'Yes, phoned it in right away but it came back as a private company car for a small accounting firm in Brussels.'

'Who the hell are these people?' Jane wondered aloud.

'I phoned into our German branch and was given the address of this safe house to use and three local agents to work with, they were all here when I arrived. I sent over all the information that you had gave me and asked them to go out and use their local knowledge to try and find out anything that might lead us to this Clarke guy, or any of his dealings in Dortmund.'

He stopped and took a drink of his coffee and checked something on his computer before he began talking again.

'There wasn't anything for the first twelve hours of any real importance — until five o'clock today when I received a voicemail message, I still have it on my phone.' He took out his mobile phone and sat it between the three of them and played the message on loudspeaker.

There was silence for five seconds then a man's voice started talking in a rushed German accent.

'Klass, it's Philip, I followed up on the intel I got from my undercover source in the police. I have been to two clubs and asked around discreetly about our man, I picked up from one bouncer that the owner spends most of his time in their biggest club, I'm outside now, I have phoned one of my team to assist, I will get back to you in an hour or two if I get anything of interest.'

The line went dead, Ryan and Jane looked at each other, then at Klass, he was clearly still thinking about what had happened. After a few seconds Jane asked him, what Ryan was about to ask himself.

'What intel did Philip get from his undercover source?'

Klass waited another few seconds, as if he were composing himself.

'He phoned me first thing this morning to let me know that one of the men he works with had heard that a young English man had been looking into purchasing a few bars and nightclubs around six months ago, no one knew who the person was — as it was all done through a local estate agent. But they said about two weeks ago — who they thought was the owner, had started showing up and setting up an office in the city somewhere. He also began to make some changes to staff, bringing in some new men behind the bar and working the doors.'

'How could this be connected?' Ryan asked.

'We're not quite sure but it seems like too much of a coincidence, plus the fact that all that shit took place in Amsterdam yesterday, meant we were keen to see what he could find out.'

Klass stopped again and stared down at his computer screen in deep thought.

'We got a call from the local police department just before I phoned you in Amsterdam, to let us know that Philip had been found with a gunshot wound in his stomach in an alley behind the club. They thought he might have been led outside, as there is only access through an emergency exit or over an eight-foot fence.'

'What about the man who was with him?' Jane asked.

'We haven't heard anything from him, but as he wasn't strictly one of ours, we don't have direct contact with him so we will have to wait and see, we have agents out there trying to track him down now.'

Jane stood up and headed over to the window.

'So, what is the plan now, can we get anywhere near the club anytime soon?' she asked.

'The local police will know he was Interpol by now, but we don't have jurisdiction to go down and start checking until they have done their checks and are happy to let anyone else in. It could be tomorrow before we get the call, when we do, we will let you both know to head down.'

Ryan was surprised, but glad he was included and could have a look around himself.

'Ok.' said Jane. 'There is no point doing anything tonight then, we would be as well getting some sleep and starting early tomorrow morning.'

Klass got up and walked over to the sink and rinsed out his coffee mug.

Ryan walked over to Jane who was still standing at the window.

'I'm going to find a hotel room close by and get some sleep, I will be back here at seven tomorrow morning, and we can get breakfast here before heading into the city.'

Jane was going to suggest he could stay here but realised it would be for the best if he didn't.

'Ok, I saw a hotel just before we turned into the complex.'

'Yeah, me too,' said Ryan. 'I will get a room there and see you in the morning.'

He said bye to Klass before heading out to the corridor and took the stairs down to the street. He buttoned his jacket up as he walked out through the glass door and out into the complex.

Chapter 22

Michael had just received an encrypted email updating him on all that had happened on the case. He knew Ryan had called about the slim guy who they had discovered was called Clarke, and although they had many resources at their disposal, they couldn't come up with any leads regarding him. The latest addition to the case was that Jones had been given permission to head out to Amsterdam to assist, Michael found this strange and took out his phone to call head office to get clarification, as he was not sure why they were doing this — when they had nothing as of yet, to assist on.

***

Ryan walked past the hotel he said he was getting a room in and made his way for the nightclub. He checked the location on his phone and knew it was only a twenty-minute walk. He wasn't planning on entering the club or obviously being spotted before going in tomorrow, but he wanted to get his bearings and check the layout of the building.

He walked fast but not rushed; his plan was to circle the building a few times. It took him eighteen minutes to get there, probably because he was so cold. He approached the club from the south, which sat on the left-hand side of a busy road. The club was empty, but the street was very busy, there was a number of pubs and take away shops on it; the recent murder had not deterred anyone by the looks of it. Ryan walked past on the opposite side of the street and looped round the building and came back down behind it, he could see the eight-foot fence and the alleyway from Klass' description earlier. There were three or four police standing inside but the body had been taken away. He came out from the side of the club — two buildings up from it, but this time he walked past on the same side of the road. There were two police standing at the entrance with what looked like a couple of workers behind them.

He could see other people inside who looked like more police, except for one man who was standing off to the left, he didn't fit in, and Ryan got the feeling that he had seen him somewhere before, but he couldn't think from where.

He didn't want to risk another walk by, so he stopped at a takeaway shop and got some food, to try and blend in, just in case someone was watching him.

He left the shop and headed back to the hotel but on a different route again. He tossed the food in the nearest bin and hurried to the hotel. He got the lift to the first floor and found his room; it was similar in layout to the hotel he'd stayed in yesterday. He stripped off, showered, and climbed into bed, all the time trying to remember where he had seen the man from the club before.

***

Sonny couldn't sleep but last night in particular, was pretty bad. The bed he slept on wasn't actually that bad, but it was more the anticipation — mixed with anxiety, which had kept him awake staring at the ceiling of his temporary prison cell. He hoped and imagined that the team would awake at first light, if they were in fact going ahead with moving him onto another location. They would discuss their plan over coffee before getting the finer details ironed out, just before they planned to move. Sonny looked at his watch that they kindly let him keep when they took all his other belongings, it was 7:45, hopefully it would be soon, he lay back down on his bed, and waited.

***

Jones was in Calais early that morning and was already eating breakfast at the terminal café when Clarke's man arrived to pick him up, his name was Peter. He was mid-thirties, just over six feet tall with brown hair, going grey on the sides. Jones knew he was the guy that managed a lot of the clubs and operations in Holland and Germany for Sonny.

He joined Jones at his table and ordered coffee and a bagel. He told Jones that they were tight for time, he had arranged to meet the customs officer on the way to pick Jones up but got a call to say he was held up, so they would need to take their coffee with them.

'We're meeting him in ten minutes.' Peter said.

Clarke had already been on the phone to him twice making sure that there wouldn't be any problems at their end. Jones paid their bill and they headed out to Peter's car. He was driving a Ford Ranger 4x4 that was parked at the front door, the car was still warm. Peter had left Dortmund at 1:00 a.m. and had driven all night without stopping. They left the car park — drove out of the terminal and made their way for the motorway.

It took them just over fifteen minutes to reach the lay-by. The car they were looking for was a beat-up old Renault Clio. Peter parked the car and waited for a signal before he got out. Although it was cold, Jones had managed to put his window down a little just before Peter switched the engine off, he wanted to try and hear what he could, as he had been told on the drive from the terminal to stay in the car.

Peter got out and the man in the Clio opened his door and strolled over to the front of their jeep, they never bothered with small talk.

'We have another container coming through in the next forty-eight hours, not sure when exactly, but when we do, you will be told the details,' said Peter.

'Ok,' the customs man replied.

'I know we say this with all the containers we use through here but this time there is no way it can be stopped; this one is of the highest importance.'

The customs man shuffled his feet and looked about nervously for a second. He had been doing this for eight months and knew it could get him jailed or even worse. He composed himself before he spoke.

'Yes, I know, we haven't had any problems so far and I will make sure there are none with this shipment either.'

'This may be our last one for a while, so we have tripled your money. We might be starting it again in a few months, but this is a goodwill gesture incase it's a little longer.' Peter lied; this one would be their last. At least Sonny hoped.

'Ok, thanks, I will make sure we have no problems.'

Peter shook his hand as he passed him the briefcase, he got back in the car and started the engine and put the car into first gear.

'I don't trust that guy,' he sneered before pulling away.

Chapter 23

Ryan had woken just after 6:00 a.m. He opened his eyes and stretched. After falling asleep last night thinking about the man from the club, he was now sitting on the end of his hotel bed — still thinking about him, and still not able to remember his face. He must have glanced at him in passing somewhere recently. He put it to the back of his mind for now and got up and headed for the bathroom, he brushed his teeth and took a long boiling hot shower, today could possibly be a long day and he planned on having a good breakfast when he got to the apartment. He thought about Jane for a second before turning off the shower and lifting his towel. He wrapped it round him and walked over to the desk in his room, his phone was lit up with a voicemail message. He picked it up and opened it, it was from Michael.

'Ryan it's Michael, I have had an update on the case as I'm sure you have too. I need to meet up as soon as possible to find out what you have found and see where you are with any lead's, phone me when you get this.'

The message ended and Ryan began to get ready. He knew he had to report back, but right now he wanted to concentrate on the case here in Dortmund and get into the nightclub, with help from Klass and see what he could get from it before he told Michael he was even in Dortmund.

He left the hotel and onto the street. The sky was clear as he made his way to the apartment block, it was only a five-minute walk, but he was frozen by the time he got buzzed into the luxurious lobby and took the lift immediately to the fifth floor. He knocked on the door and waited a few seconds before it was opened, Jane smiled at him and turned heading for the breakfast bar.

'Good morning, how are you today?' she asked.

'Fine thanks, had a good sleep and looking forward to a good breakfast.' Ryan replied.

'Klass has nipped out to pick it up from a café the local guys use, he should be back in five.'

'Great, how are you this morning?' Ryan asked.

'I'm fine, had a good sleep too and a long shower.'

Ryan smiled to himself, he thought about his own shower then thought about Jane having her shower, probably at the same time. She wasn't looking as professional as she had the last few days. She was wearing fitted jeans with a turn up at the bottom and a pair of running trainers that still looked stylish, she had a white t-shirt with a sporty grey hoodie over the top. She still looked good, Ryan thought as he took a seat at the breakfast bar.

They both sat for a minute before Jane asked.

'Did you find out anything of interest last night when you left?'

Ryan looked at her for a second.

'Did one of you follow me?' he replied slightly annoyed.

'No, of course not, I just knew that there was no way you were going straight to a hotel when you left here last night. Did you go and check out the club?' she continued.

Ryan should have known she would have figured out what he would be doing.

'Yes, I circled the club twice, the second time I walked right past the front entrance and had a good look in.'

'Did anything stand out?'

'The body had been taken away from the alley but there were still some police standing around, forensics must have left by then.'

Jane nodded.

'When I passed the entrance, I caught a glimpse of a

man in the club, he didn't look like he was from the police and I am sure that I have seen his face before, but I can't think from where, but he has stuck in my mind.'

'If you can give us a description, we can run it through our system and see if anyone jumps out.'

Ryan described the man he saw, and Jane sent it to what Ryan assumed, would be their head office for someone to check against their records.

She sat back in her stool and turned to Ryan about to say something but was interrupted by the sound of keys rattling in the apartment door lock. Both of them looked round as Klass came in with one of the agents behind him, they were both carrying a paper bag that Ryan hoped was hot food.

It was, Jane poured the four of them fresh orange juice in clear glasses and sat them out for everyone. They had gotten the works, hot croissants, pastries, and fresh rolls with what looked like freshly cooked meat. Ryan ate as much as he could without seeming rude. Klass then made everyone coffee before they all sat at the breakfast bar to discuss what the plan was for the day.

Ryan took a sip of his coffee and started talking first.

'When I left here last night, I took a walk into town before heading to the hotel.'

Everyone looked at him as if to elaborate further.

'I walked up to the club from the south before circling the building twice, I explained to Jane before you got here that I saw the alleyway where your agent had been killed, before walking past the front entrance. I wanted to get an idea of the location before we get in there today, if we do.'

'Did you see anything of interest?' Klass asked Ryan even though he was a little annoyed that he had took the risk of going to the club without them, but he knew he didn't have any authority over him.

'As I described to Jane, I saw a man inside that I thought I had seen recently but I can't remember from were exactly.'

Klass and the other agent looked at Jane.

'I took a description from him and sent it to head office, hopefully in the next hour or two we will hear something back,' she told them.

'Ok.' Klass said. Then began. 'We heard from our local chief that the head of the police department has contacted him this morning to let them know we have an hour in the nightclub at 10 a.m. We have told them that Ryan is from British intelligence and has clearance to assist us in the investigation, they don't need to know anymore at this point. We will be leaving at 9:30 a.m. and can all go in our car, Jane will need to meet with our section chief before we go in, no doubt. Hopefully, we get a hit back on the description Ryan gave Jane this morning before we head over there, so we can make enquiries into him.'

***

Sonny could hear a little more commotion than usual coming from outside. He sat up on his bed and spun his legs around, he already had his boots on. He tried to listen but couldn't make out any of the conversations, so he stood and walked up to the door to listen closer. He could tell that it was one voice that was doing most of the talking, probably someone giving out orders and explaining the plan to the men again. After a few minutes he gave up and started to pace up and down his makeshift cell, knowing that something was hopefully going to happen soon. He needed out of this room as soon as possible; he was going crazy. His jacket was still hanging on the back of a chair that sat at a desk, on the opposite side of the room to the door, he walked over and took it, he put it on and buttoned it up before looking in the mirror that was stuck to the wall just to the right of the desk, and smiled.

Nearly there he said quietly to himself, at the exact same time that his cell door was kicked in and three men rushed through. The leading guy putting a bag over his head as the other two grabbed him by the arms and dragged him out of the room.

***

Jones was doing most of the talking on the drive to Amsterdam. They were sitting on the motorway at 90 kilometers per hour and had been driving for just over three hours. They were expected to reach the city Centre around 9:45 a.m. that day; they were almost through Belgium and would be crossing into Holland soon.

Jones had been trying to get more information, but Peter wasn't really a talkative guy. He had spoken of a nightclub in Dortmund that Clarke had been using as a base over the last two weeks but didn't elaborate, to Jones' annoyance.

'So is Clarke still in Dortmund now, or has he made his way back to Amsterdam yet?'

'Still in Dortmund when I left last night but he was looking to get moving early this afternoon.' Peter replied.

Jones was hoping to finally meet him today, as his only contact with him up to now had been through phone or email.

***

After an hour going over everything again and drinking more coffee, Klass had decided to head for the club early, and hopefully get inside a little sooner. Ryan and Jane were sitting in the car waiting on him to come down.

'You've been quiet the last hour, everything ok?' Jane asked.

'The man I described to you earlier is playing on my mind, I think I know where I saw him, but his face isn't totally clear in my mind.'

'Where do you think it was?'

'When I left the stadium yesterday and was walking to the station there was a man standing in a bar that I passed. He wasn't looking out at me, and I could only see the side of his face but I'm positive it was the same guy.'

'Could it be a coincidence?' Jane said.

'The fact that he was there, but not inside the stadium watching the game, I would say not. I just wonder how long he has been watching me, or if he still is.'

Jane began thinking back. 'I can't recall, but at the same time I can't be sure.'

'I'm positive I haven't noticed him before or since then.' Ryan said a little unsure.

'Hopefully, our tech guys get a hit soon and we can look into it more. I will say to them to try and pull CCTV from around the stadium and maybe get an image of him, but it could take time.'

Ryan nodded just as Klass opened the door and sat in the passenger seat. He turned around to face Ryan and Jane who were sitting in the back and said. 'We have a problem.'

Chapter 24

'When we got to the café to pick up breakfast earlier, Jari thought he noticed a car parked in the next street along that he had also noticed just after we left the complex. He thought it seemed suspicious so as he went to collect the food I called in the registration. I just received a call back saying that the car is registered to a small accounting firm from Brussels.'

'Shit!' Jane said, annoyed.

'They must have been on us since we arrived in Dortmund, possibly even Amsterdam,' said Ryan.

'It also means that the safe house isn't very safe anymore, or maybe never has been,' said Klass.

'So, what do we do know?' Jane inquired.

Klass spoke after a few minutes of silence.

'As far as they know we haven't spotted them yet, so I think for now we carry on to the club, as normal, and play along.'

'You sure?' Jane asked.

'He's right.' Ryan cut in. 'They will know by now that both of you are Interpol and I'm positive they will know who I am, especially if they have been on me since the stadium.'

'I agree,' said Klass.

'So, like Klass said we carry on as normal and think of the best way to deal with them when we get there.'

Klass put the VW Tiguan into gear and pulled away from the apartment complex and out onto the street.

Ryan now knew that they were well behind and felt a little under pressure that he still wasn't making any headway into what was going on. It had been two days since he had arrived in Amsterdam. He needed to contact Michael and discover if he had any new leads and maybe lure anyone who might be watching them, out into the open.

***

Clarke had left Dortmund and been driving for over an hour when his phone rang.

'They have left the safe house and are heading in the direction of the club; we are well back and are pretty sure we haven't been spotted. They also have our friend from Amsterdam riding with them, I will keep you updated.'

Clarke hung up the phone and called Peter.

Peter's phone began to ring but instead of answering through the Bluetooth in the car, he picked it out of his pocket and put it to his ear.

'Yes,' he answered.

'Interpol are on their way to the club, and they have our friend along for the ride, where are you?'

'We have just come into the city Centre, ten minutes away.' Peter replied.

'Ok, dump Jones and carry onto the club but be careful. Is the package still secure?'

'Yes.'

'Good, I will be in touch when we want you to move out.'

Jones could only make out parts of the conversation, but knew something had changed.

***

Ryan was in the back of the car thinking hard about what their next move should be. He was positive that they would have switched the car from this morning just to be safe, so everyone was on the lookout for a new car that could be following them.

Jane spotted it just over halfway to the club, it was a

black VW golf GTI, it had two passengers and was sitting five cars back from them. They gave themselves away when Klass turned up a side street off the main road, intentionally, which they followed, before rejoining further on up the road the same as Klass.

They carried on driving at a normal pace and five minutes from the club Ryan told them his plan.

'I don't need to go into the club, you guys know what you're looking for and I saw what I needed to last night. I think there is more to gained by seeing what happens from outside the club.'

Klass and Jane both agreed.

The plan was — at a set of traffic lights that Ryan had noticed last night, behind the club, he would get Klass to drive through the red light and turn left and then loop back around, where Ryan would jump out and head down a street running parallel to the club. Hopefully not being seen by the GTI, from there he could cross the road in front of the club when the car that was following them had passed by and watch from the café opposite.

They carried on still trying to keep a gap between the GTI and themselves to give Ryan his opportunity. The car was dodging through the traffic to try and keep up. They passed the front of the club and approached the lights just as they were changing from green to red and Klass hit the accelerator and sped through them. The chasing car saw this and tried to follow but wasn't quick enough. Klass had looped round and was at the back of the club; he jumped on the brakes and Ryan quickly got out and ran down the side street and hid himself in the doorway of a restaurant. He looked out and back to where he had come to see the black Golf GTI passing by at speed. He stepped out from the doorway, crossed the street, and entered a café opposite the club, he sat by the window and waited.

Chapter 25

Sonny could feel the sweat on his forehead. Even although he was sure that his men were reliable and everything would go to plan, he was still anxious. After he was dragged from his cell, they had marched him for fifty yards before he came out into the sunlight, he could see the sun shining through the bag over his head. No one spoke as he was being put into the back of what he thought would be the same jeep that he had been driven here in thirty-six hours earlier. The car sped away as soon as his door was slammed shut and he was thrown back into his seat. He knew he was in the middle between what he could tell, with the space he had, were two big men. At this point he wasn't sure yet if any of them were the guy that Clarke had managed to flip, he would find out soon enough though. He closed his eyes knowing the plan was in action and the thought of finally being free. The car turned off the dirt road and headed west, in the opposite direction from Amsterdam.

***

Jones got out of the car and Peter pulled away. He was starting to feel uneasy as he walked towards Dortmund city Centre, now he knew that meeting Clarke today was unlikely, he wasn't sure what to do next.

He stopped off at a bar and sat in the beer garden and ordered a lager, he opened his laptop and started writing an email to Michael. He still wanted to keep his cover as long as he could and needed to let them know that he'd had a tip off and was making his way to Dortmund to check up on it, before heading onto Amsterdam.

***

Ryan was watching from the café as the black VW golf passed by slowly. Klass had stopped the car right in front of the club and got out; they were now standing on the pavement outside. Jane was speaking to a small man with a ponytail who he assumed must be her section leader, they had been standing for a few minutes moving from side to side in the cold to keep warm. Not long after they got the go ahead, Jane pushed open the huge glass doors and entered the foyer area.

The club was busy with people who looked mostly like law enforcement and a few staff workers. By now everyone would have combed the scene and all the forensics would have been taken, Jane and Klass felt like they were being fed the scraps. When they had finished with their section leader Jane headed out to the alleyway where the body had been found. The body had been removed but the outline of where it had lay was still visible, she had a look at the fence and the area outside to see if there was anything of interest, but it all looked normal, as far as she could see. Klass was still inside, he was talking to the officer in charge of the crime scene, he was a large man by the name of Frenkie and he looked stressed. Klass was hoping to get some CCTV footage or access to any witnesses from the night before, that they would be able to question but he struck out on both counts. After a few minutes of getting nowhere, he went out to speak to Jane.

'The fence is secure,' said Jane.

Klass looked the fence up and down.

'So, whoever did this you are sure must have entered this area and left again through the club?'

'Yeah, I'm pretty sure,' Jane continued 'how did you get on inside?'

'CCTV has been down since last weekend.'

Jane smirked and shook her head.

'Everyone who was stopped leaving the club yesterday says that they never saw anything, and if this place is owned by who we think it could be owned by, there is no way *any* of them were going to talk, if they saw anything or not.'

They both headed back inside and asked if the owner had been contacted and questioned yet. They were told he hadn't but the general manager of the club, Peter, who was here last night but left half an hour before the man was killed and returned for a short time afterwards, was on his way to speak to the local police.

'When is he due?' asked Klass a little pissed that he still hadn't been questioned.

'Any minute,' replied the officer.

***

Ryan was still sitting in the café across the street, and he was starting to get impatient, he wished he had gone into the club after all. He had caught a few glimpses of Jane and Klass through the big glass doors, they had split up briefly but were now standing in what Ryan would have assumed was the dance floor, talking to a large man with a local police uniform on. He got to his feet and decided to head over to the club and join them, when a 4X4 pickup truck pulled up to the kerb at the entrance of the club. Ryan waited and stood at the café window and watched as a man of average height and build got out of the car. Ryan could only see him from the side as he headed straight into the club. He was quickly approached by the man in the uniform that was talking with Jane and Klass and taken to one side where a woman who looked like a detective came over and joined them, followed by Jane and Klass. They were taking a seat, maybe to begin questioning him. Ryan thought.

After ten minutes of meandering near the door of the café. Ryan saw the man from the pickup reappear from the club and go to his car. Ryan couldn't see his face clearly though and as he was just about to jump into the 4X4, something caught his attention. He appeared to say something before stepping out of the car again, just as another man came into view. The second man was walking across the road, facing away from Ryan. Ryan opened the café door and stepped out; he started making his way towards the men when his mobile phone started ringing in his pocket. He fished it out and looked at the screen, it was Jane, he put it back in his pocket and carried on towards them. He was twenty feet from them when his mobile started to ring again, but this time he was close enough for the men to hear the ring. The second man that had walked across the road turned around first, it was Jones, the contact he met in the alleyway in Edinburgh three nights ago, he looked shocked to see Ryan but tried his best to keep his composure. Jones opened his mouth to speak but from off his left shoulder, the man Jones had been approaching came into view, and Ryan started sprinting, but the man had reacted just as fast. He was in the car and had it running as Ryan got close to it, he hit the accelerator and sped away, Ryan punched at the passenger side window, but his hand bounced off it, he kept running though, and hauled the huge glass door open and roared inside.

'Get to the car, now!'

Jane and Klass ran out and scrambled into the car. Ryan was already in the passenger seat as they both got into their seats and sped away in pursuit of the pickup truck.

The road was busy in front of them, and they could only see the top of the car in the distance, but Ryan had caught the registration plate 'ERH V605' and he was repeating it to Jane who was sitting in the back already on her phone, trying to get through to head office.

'What's going on?' she asked waiting to be put through to another department.

'The guy you were talking to inside the club, that's the guy I described to you both, the one I think has been following me.'

'Seriously?' said Jane.

Klass was weaving in and out of traffic as best he could but it was not helping, and he couldn't seem to gain on the pickup.

'I never even clicked,' said Jane still on hold.

They were now out of the City Centre and heading onto a bypass that was taking them north, the car seemed to be getting further away with every minute. Jane began talking in the back and gave whoever was on the other side of the phone the registration number, she waited for a few minutes and hung up the phone.

'Guess!' She said.

'Small accounting firm?' Said Klass.

'Yip,' she replied.

Ryan shouted as he punched the dash of the car.

He told Klass to go as fast as he could, but the pickup was almost out of sight. They drove on frantically for another five minutes before they lost him completely. They turned around at the next slip road — heading back to Dortmund.

It took them twenty minutes to get back to the club. They were annoyed and frustrated. Ryan had asked Jane as they turned around to phone someone from her section to make sure that Jones was kept under supervision until they got back, and they could question him. When she had ended her call, Ryan took his mobile phone out and phoned Michael, he wasn't looking forward to making the call, as he had five messages from him already.

Michael answered on the first ring.

'Jesus Christ Ryan, what the hell is going on?'

'Sorry, since I left you at the stadium it's been hectic.'

'That's no excuse, I've left you five messages and phoned a thousand times!'

'We found out that one of Interpol's men was killed in Dortmund in a club which is owned by a person of interest in our case,'

'Dortmund.' Michael said angrily.

'I know, I should have told you sooner, but I haven't had the chance, we jumped on the earliest train we could and got here yesterday.'

Ryan then explained the events which led them there. The details of the murder and the man that he was sure was following him since he landed in Amsterdam, and how he had appeared outside the club where the killing took place. At that point he realised that he still hadn't spoken to Jane or Klass yet about the guy in the pickup and what was said in the club.

'Then something strange happened,' Ryan continued.

'What now?' replied Michael.

'When I was about to head over to meet Jane in the club, I saw one of our guys standing outside talking to the guy I just told you about, the one we chased after.'

'One of our guys?' Michael thought for a second. 'Who was it?'

'Jones,' said Ryan.

'Why the hell is Jones out there, the last I heard was that he was on his way to meet with us in Amsterdam, how did he know you were in Dortmund?'

'I'm not sure he did,'

'I'm going to have to make some more calls on him, something doesn't add up, in the meantime keep him close.'

'I have someone with eyes on him now and I will

question him when I get back and let you know.' Replied Ryan.

'You better,' said Michael.

'Promise,' said Ryan and he hung up the phone.

Chapter 26

Michael dialed the London office when he got off the phone with Ryan. He waited on hold for a few minutes before being put through to the chief of the department.

He knew Jones had been given permission to go to Amsterdam already, this had been confirmed, but they did say that they hadn't received confirmation yet of him arriving. Michael explained to the chief that he had turned up in Dortmund instead and asked his chief if they were aware of this, which they were not, and before ending the call, told Michael that they would look into it.

Michael then phoned Ryan to let him know what he had found out and how Jones hadn't been updating his chief in London. They both decided to keep an even closer eye on him for now, and for Ryan to go easy on him when he got back.

Jones was being held in one of Interpol's local depots. Ryan, Jane and Klass, all went in to hear what he had to say. The building was pretty old looking from the outside, like an old police station or courthouse. When they got inside, they were shown to a conference room near the back, where Jones was sitting looking very worried, sipping on a cup of coffee.

Ryan came in first and Jones stood up and shook his hand.

'How's things?' Jones said nervously.

'Not great to be honest, looks like were in the middle of a shit storm at the moment and everybody seems to know what's going on except for us.' Ryan said angrily.

Jones looked down at the table before speaking.

'As you know I had been assisting on the case from London but had come to a dead end, so I thought that I would be of more use here with you.'

Ryan stared at him with no expression.

Jones continued.

'So, I got it cleared with my chief of department.'

'But how did you know I was here in Dortmund?' asked Ryan.

Jones hesitated.

'When you contacted us regarding the man you needed details on, I was told to put a trace on your mobile phone. They wanted to keep tabs on your movement in case you would require back up. We knew that you arrived here last night, so I made my way over hoping you would still be here.'

Ryan looked over at Jane who was looking at him skeptically.

'Seems like a bit of a risk to me,' said Ryan.

'If you had already left then I would have checked out a few things for myself, then carried onto Amsterdam in the morning and met up with Michael.'

'How did you know that man you were speaking to outside the club earlier?'

'I didn't.'

'Looked to me like you were familiar with each other.'

Jones tried to keep composed. 'I got an email through about the murder at the club, and with you being located so close I thought to come and check it out.'

'And the guy?'

'I saw him leave the club from across the street and assumed he was a detective, I hoped he could get me clearance to go in.'

Ryan stood up knowing that Jones was making the story up as he went along, he thought about his conversation with Michael and decided to end it. He would try to use Jones to his advantage.

'Ok, we have some new leads to work with and an extra body now so let's work together on this. I really need the name of the guy in the pickup, and we need to talk about what you guys found out in the club.' Ryan said.

They all left the station together. Ryan said to Jane and Klass about going over what they found out today, but Klass said he needed to call in to head office and type some paperwork up first, he agreed to catch up later that night and offered to drop Jones off at a local hotel.

Ryan and Jane walked slowly towards the city Centre. It was a city that Ryan hadn't been to before but looked exactly like he had imagined, bright, loud, and bustling with people, looking for dinner or a beer. They found a bar that sold food and headed inside. They both took off their jackets and ordered a beer and burger when the waitress appeared, they sat sipping them for a few minutes before Jane asked.

'What did you make of Jones' story?'

Ryan was holding his beer in both hands staring into the glass deep in thought, he looked up after a few seconds and said. 'I didn't believe a word of it.'

'Good' said Jane 'neither did I.' Just as the waitress arrived with their food.

Chapter 27

Klass never spoke on the short journey to Jones' hotel, they both clearly had things on their minds. Jones said thanks when the car stopped, and he got out.

He checked into a room on the top floor, got in and dropped his bag. The mobile phone he had with only the one number saved in it started ringing in his pocket, he took it out and looked at it, he had six missed calls from the same number, he threw the phone on the bed and lay down and closed his eyes.

***

The Volvo that Sonny had been thrown into had been traveling for forty-five minutes, he couldn't tell what direction they were going, and he really didn't care. Clarke had organised everything perfectly. So far, the car had been silent but finally he heard a voice; he assumed it was the driver saying something to the passenger, he didn't catch what he said, the passenger replied with yes and a few minutes later the car turned off a smooth road and onto one that felt more like a country road — Sonny was being thrown all over the place. The car rumbled on for ten minutes before turning sharp left and driving much slower, it stopped soon after and the driver turned the engine off. His blindfold was removed but the brightness from the sun was so blinding it took him a while to adjust his eyes. He squinted out the front window and could make out a small outhouse building on what appeared to be, the bottom corner of a field. Beyond the outhouse the sun was beginning to set, all he could see in the distance was more fields.

No one got out the car or seemed to know what to do next, they sat unsure until a figure walked out from around the back of the outhouse, it was Clarke. He slowly approached the car and signaled to the driver to lower his window, the driver did and was about to greet him when Sonny was blinded once again. Clarke, on approaching the driver's window had pulled a handgun — out of sight of everyone inside and shot the driver at point black range in the side of the head. At the same time, the passenger had spun round in his seat and shot both the men sitting on either side of Sonny, there was smoke and blood and brains everywhere. Sonny quickly jumped over one of the dead men and landed on the grass outside, he wiped what he could off himself and stretched. Clarke came around from the other side of the car and shook his hand, they looked at each other, both a little relieved.

'You did good kid,' said Sonny with a smile.

'I'm glad your back boss.' Clarke replied.

'What is the word on the street then, is anyone suspicious of the kidnap?'

'From what we have heard, everyone thinks it was genuine, even the media bought into it. They are all assuming it was a gang hit, and as far as everyone is concerned, you're as good as dead,' Clarke replied then asked, 'the plan still the same then?'

Sonny looked over at the outhouse as the sun was setting, apart from his surroundings, he thought it looked beautiful. He had gone over the plan in his head for the last few days, he had debated whether to try and flee without any more killing and hope to get away and never be found, but reality got the better of him. He took the gun from Clarke's hand and in one movement, spun round and shot the man that had helped get him out alive, in the Centre of the forehead. The man fell to the floor like someone had stolen his body from out of his clothes.

Sonny turned around again and faced Clarke. 'No one can know that I am still alive, when they find us, and they will, they need to be killed before I make my escape, I have to be sure.'

***

Jones woke up after an hour's sleep, his phone was ringing next to him, he answered it still half asleep.

'Where they hell are you? I have been trying to get a hold of you for an hour, what's going on?'

Jones had expected Clarke to be pissed. 'Quiet from what I found out today, they are still running around in circles trying to figure out what's going on,' he Replied.

'Good, where are you now?'

'I'm in my hotel getting ready to leave.' Jones replied.

'Ok.' said Clarke. 'We are now moving ahead with plan B; we need you to make the call when you're on your way.'

Jones got off the phone and walked over to the window. He stood looking out at nothing in particular, thinking how the last few months had changed his whole life and ended up with him being here, going against everything he believed in. He showered and changed before heading down to the reception and asking the lady on duty to call him a taxi.

Chapter 28

Sonny and Clarke had got the fourth body into the Volvo, which Clarke was now driving as fast as he could. Sonny was following close behind in a black Mercedes that Clarke had used to travel to the outhouse, he had parked it behind the building, so it was out of sight as the men approached. Clarke had drove the last hundred yards with his head hanging out the window, due to the smell from the dead bodies.

He pulled the car onto the verge of a slip road, half sticking out of the tress that ran up the side of the road, they wanted to make it look like it could have crashed, when it was checked over by the police later on. Sonny pulled in behind him and got out, he was carrying the can of petrol and matches that Clarke had brought from the warehouse. They pushed the car further into the trees and Sonny picked up the petrol can again and started pouring it all over the car, when it was empty, he threw it into the open window and stepped back before lighting a match and throwing it onto the roof. They didn't hang around to watch it burn, they hurried back to Clarke's car and got in, Clarke driving this time. They pulled off the slip road and headed south. Sonny was now sitting in the passenger seat of the black Mercedes, stretched out. The sun had set as he looked in the rear-view mirror, all he could see in the darkness was the orange flames, dancing against the night sky.

***

Klass was parked fifty yards up the street from the front of the hotel, he had found a space behind a bakery truck that kept him well hidden. The sun had set ten minutes ago, and he had been sitting for so long he was beginning to get tired, and hungry, and bored. After dropping Jones off earlier he started thinking about his story back in the conference room. It had been so full of holes that it had annoyed him, he assumed Ryan and Jane felt the same, but he thought better of telling them what he thought just yet, it could be sensitive because at the end of the day he was working for the same intelligence agency as Ryan. So, when he dropped Jones off, he decided to circle the block and keep an eye on him, and anyone else coming or going from his hotel, and so far, three couples and a man in his fifties had entered, who was possibly a worker, but that was it.

He was getting ready to call it a night when he finally saw Jones appear from the hotel reception, Klass wasn't sure whether to get out or not until a taxi pulled up and Jones got in. Klass pulled his seatbelt on and started the car, feeling good about the fact that something was finally happening.

***

Ryan and Jane finished their meal and had stayed in the bar talking for a bit longer. They decided to head back to Jane's. They buttoned up before making their way to the square, it was freezing and packed as they hustled their way through the crowds.

***

The taxi Jones got in was a new Skoda estate and was driving the way taxi drivers usually did, slow and steady for maximum fuel efficiency, which made Klass fairly confident that he could stay far back and not be spotted. He had noticed before he got into the taxi, that Jones had changed his clothes from when he had dropped him off earlier, but he was still carrying his shoulder bag that must have had a laptop inside.

The Skoda meandered its way out of Dortmund city Centre and headed southwest on to the 52 road, he knew the driver wouldn't be looking out for someone following the car, but he also thought if Jones was as smart as he should be, even he would have realised that his story from earlier was going to arouse some suspicion. So, when they got up to 80 kph, Klass dropped back to a hundred yards behind and settled in for the possibility of a long drive.

***

Jane's section leader was sitting at his desk. He was alone in the office as he had sent everyone else home at 9 p.m. — he told them to get some rest as tomorrow looked like it could be a busy day, they had to follow up leads and hit the streets for information, he didn't want this getting out of control. The main reason for him staying back though was to have a better look into that guy Jones and also, go over Ryan's files again. He made a call to headquarters for access to the file that had been made up three days ago, when Jane had phoned in to say she was working with an agent from a department of British Intelligence, she needed clearance to do so.

Ryan's file was on his screen along with a picture and everything looked ok. His full name was Ryan Snow, middle name Joseph. He was born in Britain, but the exact location was undisclosed, he currently lived in Scotland, with no town given and he had done for the past four years. According to the file he was twenty-nine-years old and had been in the agency from just after his twentieth birthday, it says he was raised by his gran as his mother died when he was young, his dad had looked after him until he was eleven. It also mentioned that when he joined the agency to begin with, he was part of a unit that only a few years after Ryan joined had been investigated, and almost all of them were removed from the agency altogether. Ryan was one of the few that wasn't, instead he was transferred to a new department. Interpol had found nothing to worry about from his background and so he was cleared to work with them in this case, but they did require regular updates from Jane regarding their progress, and so far, she had done this. He then pulled up Jones' file, which had no picture or clearance and only told them he was an agent of a department of British Intelligence. He closed the file and turned off his computer, just as his office phone began to ring, loudly in the empty office.

'Hello?' He answered quickly.

The person on the other side of the phone never introduced himself.

'We believe that someone from this office has recently been dealing with two people of interest from British Intelligence.'

'That's correct,' replied the section leader. 'Who am I speaking with?' he asked.

'We are informing you that both these men are no longer acting on behalf of the agency, they have been instructed to hand themselves in immediately.'

'I need to know who I am speaking with please?'

'We strongly advise that they are detained, and your officer who has been assisting one of the agents be held for questioning. We will be in touch in the near future.'

The phone went dead, the section leader slammed down the receiver and brought up Ryan's file again. He then picked up the phone again to call his boss with this information when the buzzer for the front door sounded, he clicked off the file and brought up the outside camera, it was Jane and Ryan.

Chapter 29

Jones hung up the burner phone he bought at Calais and thought he had handled the call pretty well; the section leader at Interpol hadn't been part of his interview earlier, so he didn't need to change his voice. He was aware that being caught by Ryan in Dortmund wasn't ideal, and the story he had come up with was plausible but at the same time not very convincing, so when Clarke told them that they were now following plan B he was more than happy. That plan was now for Jones to try and delay Ryan as much as possible until they had moved the package, got themselves into position at the warehouse and then try and get him to follow their tracks, preferably on his own. They did not want Interpol snooping around as well as British Intelligence. He was now making his way to the bar in Düsseldorf to meet with Peter, where they would be told how and when to proceed.

***

Klass was close enough to the taxi to see the screen of Jones mobile phone lighting up, he counted roughly three minutes that he was on a call, he wondered who it could be with. There was no way he would be discussing details of the case or plans in front of a taxi driver, not unless the taxi was pre-planned, and he knew him.

The Skoda finally signaled and exited the 52 road at the junction for the city of Düsseldorf, Klass was fifty yards back and sped up slightly to make sure he didn't lose him. They passed straight through the first two roundabouts, then took the third exit at the next which took them west and heading for the north of the city. After a slow twenty-five minutes Klass pulled over as the taxi stopped and Jones got out, he could see him paying the driver and saying something to him before closing the door and walking briskly across the road. Klass hurried and grabbed his jacket and scarf from the back seat, he jogged across the road, putting them on as he did, keen to keep pace with Jones. He slowed as he got to the corner of the street that Jones walked down, he looked around, no sign of him but it was busy, it was lined on both sides, mainly with bars with a lot of people hanging around outside. He hurried again and pushed through the groups of people, he was starting to worry that he had lost him when he finally caught site of the back of his head, turning right and heading into a backstreet. Klass ran to the corner and peered round to see Jones going through a back gate at the rear of what he thought was a pub, he walked up cautiously to the fence and saw Jones being let into a side door by a man who's face he just missed, before slamming the door closed.

***

Peter was restless and it showed when he let Jones into the pub. He had made his way to Düsseldorf only after he had managed to lose the car that had chased him from the club in Dortmund. He pointed towards a back room that Jones stepped into and removed his coat and took a seat.

Peter sat a beer down in front of him and took a sip of his own.

'What the hell took you so long?' he asked angrily.

'Taxi driver wouldn't go over eighty, I told him I would pay him more to speed up, but he wouldn't have it.'

Peter looked across the room annoyed, mostly from thinking about the club earlier. Jones had almost got him caught but he knew that Clarke had spoken to him about it, and he didn't want to start on him either.

'Have you heard from them recently?' Peter asked him, knowing he had.

'Clarke phoned me before I left the hotel, he told me that we are moving to plan B.' Jones replied.

'Why?'

'I can only imagine that the two days Sonny has been locked up, he has been thinking things over and decided that he doesn't want to leave anything to chance,' Jones took a sip of his beer and continued, 'he told me to call Interpol to try and get them to hold the both of them up in Dortmund for as long as they can, we know they can't hold Ryan forever, but hopefully he will drop the woman and come alone. We now have to leave a trail of breadcrumbs when we leave here later and hope that he picks them up and eventually walks right into Sonny's hands, back in Holland.'

'I still don't know why we just don't send a guy to take him out now,' said Peter.

'Sonny knows that he can trust certain people, but when it comes to this, he needs to be their when it happens, or better still be the one who pulls the trigger, same goes with the package.'

Peter looked over at the door and thought about what Jones had just said.

'How is the package?' Jones asked.

'Same as before, hasn't said much yet, but I'm sure he has a lot to think about.'

They both took a sip of their beer.

Chapter 30

Klass knew he had to phone Jane and let her know where he was. He still wasn't sure what following Jones might lead to — if anything. It was more the fact that he was now in Düsseldorf in pursuit of Jones that he knew he had to report back to her before going any further. He took out his phone and called her number, it rang out for a minute before going to voicemail 'shit' he said to himself and put the phone back in his pocket.

He thought better of trying to get closer to the rear door as he was positive it would have CCTV, although from his position at the end of the alleyway he couldn't see a camera. He walked back down to the Main Street and checked out the front of the pub. It was an older pub and from the outside looked busy, again he couldn't see any cameras, but he was sure they would have them. He had no option now but to head inside and try get eyes on Jones again, he buttoned his coat up and pulled his hat as low as he could and walked through the groups of people at the front doors and went inside. The bar was busy, mostly with groups of young people, there was also a few couples sat at tables near the back.

Klass made his way to the bar, a teenage girl with a red Mohican haircut spotted him and asked what she could get him. He ordered a lager and waited on her pouring it, he looked through the back but there wasn't much to see. Apart from the girl serving him there was a man in his early twenties washing glasses, behind the bar to the left was a corridor with a door at the far end that was closed, there was no sign of Jones or the man who had let him in; the barman who was washing the glasses was too young from what Klass saw of him at the back door earlier. He turned and looked for a seat when the girl had served his drink, he found a booth near the back and sat down, he kept his jacket on but took off his hat, he needed to find out what Jones was doing here and could do nothing now but wait.

***

Ryan and Jane were buzzed in, eventually. They were both freezing from standing so long and the heat inside was welcomed. They headed towards the main office and Jane found the section leader at his desk.

'Hey boss,' she said, 'we're heading to the conference room to look into a few things if that's ok, we want to look into Jones who we interviewed earlier, do you have a copy of his file?'

'I think so, I will bring it in,' he replied.

'Thanks,' she said, and they headed for the conference room. Ryan nodding to him as they passed.

Someone had cleaned it from earlier, there was a smell of bleach and cleaning products when they entered. Jane took a seat at the computer and fired it up, Ryan poured them both a coffee and sat at the table next to her.

'I think you should look into the file on the nightclub murder first and to see if there are any updates or leads, before checking the file on Jones when we get it.'

Jane brought the case up and read through it, the only addition she could see was the interview that was taken with the club manager that Jane was part of, but nothing else since. She closed the computer, turned around and lifted her coffee cup.

'I have tried to phone Michael twice, and left a message, the more I think about Jones the more I think it really doesn't make any sense, I need to get eyes on him as soon as possible.' Ryan said.

Just at that the section leader opened the door of the conference room.

'I'm having trouble getting access to Jones file, but it should be cleared soon.'

'Ok.' Jane replied slightly confused. She felt her phone vibrate in her pocket, she quickly glanced at it, it was Klass, she ignored it for now and let the section leader finish.

'I received a call earlier from head office, they have come across some evidence from the nightclub and are keen to speak to you both, they have asked if you can wait here until they arrive.'

Ryan and Jane looked at each other. 'Sure, when will they get here?' Jane asked.

'Within the hour.' He replied.

He turned and left the room, Ryan thought about what he had just been told, and wasn't convinced.

'Why would there be evidence just found out but not added to the case file and why would they ask for me to stay, I never went into the nightclub?'

'Maybe because they know we are working closely on this.'

Ryan was about to reply when his mobile phone started ringing, he took it out and answered it, it was Michael. 'Hi Michael.'

'Ryan, I got your message, we're still trying to get eyes on Jones but can't even contact him to be honest,' he paused 'the reason I'm phoning is we just received a call from Interpol asking about your clearance and protocol on this case. We found it strange as we already cleared you days ago to work alongside them, when we questioned it, they avoided our question and ended the call abruptly.'

'That makes some sense now of what just happened here.' Ryan replied. 'Something seems to be going on. Thanks Michael, I will be in touch soon.'

Ryan stood up and told Jane they had to leave,

'someone is trying to keep us here, for some reason, we have to go.'

They got up and headed for the front door, but we're stopped before they could reach it by the section leader.

'Where are you going, you have been asked to stay here?'

'I don't have to do anything you ask me!' Ryan replied.

'I think it's in your best interest to stay.'

Ryan went to leave — the man stood in front of him and put his hand against Ryan's chest to prevent him from going any further. 'You're not going anywhere.'

Ryan looked over at Jane and said, 'I would rather you came with me but I'm not staying,' she nodded, and Ryan grabbed the man's arm and spun it round and put it halfway up his back, the guy shrieked in pain. At the same time Jane reached over to the desk and unlocked the front door, she walked round both men and opened the door. Ryan let go of the man's arm and followed her out.

'You know what this means?' she said to Ryan.

'Yes, we have lost all help from Interpol.'

'Exactly, but maybe not Klass.' She remembered his call and took out her phone.

'You going to phone him?'

'Yes, he called when we were being asked to stay put earlier, I ignored it.'

She dialed his number and stood looking at the sky, after a few seconds she hung it up.

'It's going straight to voicemail…' she said.

***

Klass took out his phone again to see if Jane had tried to return his call, but he had lost reception when he had entered the pub.

Chapter 31

Peter finished his beer and stood up from the table, Jones was still drinking his. He was even more restless and knew what the plan was but hated waiting around to be told when to put it into action. He walked over to the door that led to the basement where the package was being held, he opened it and looked in, nothing had changed, it would be pretty difficult for it to change with the restraints they had put on him, but he was still alive at least. He closed the door again and walked round the room a few times before sitting back down on his seat.

'They need to hurry this up.' Peter said.

'You want me to phone them?' Replied Jones.

Peter glanced at his watch. 'Leave it another half hour.'

***

Ryan and Jane made their way in the direction of the city Centre, he phoned Michael back when they were far enough away from the station.

'Michael, the call you received earlier on today that you mentioned, we are pretty sure had something to do with Interpol. I was in one of their Dortmund offices and was asked by the section leader to stay put, he said that one of his bosses was on his way with new information that he wanted to run past myself and Jane, when I said I couldn't, he got agitated and tried to physically stop me.'

'Is he ok?' Michael asked.

'Yes, I just got myself free from his grip, Jane thought something was strange with it too and decided to leave with me.'

'Ok, that's her call.' Michael replied.

Michael then took a few seconds; Ryan assumed it

was to think.

'Firstly, I will call this into to head office in London and get someone to try and find out if orders have come from higher up the chain that I am not aware of. In the meantime, I will organise a car for you to make your way back to Amsterdam, without Interpol helping, it could become tricky.'

'Yes, I know, thanks, if anything else changes I will be in touch.' Ryan said and hung up the phone.

***

Sonny and Clarke had reached the warehouse and hidden the Mercedes they had been driving, around the back in a lock-up that was always left empty. Sonny made a call for the warehouse manager Ross to meet him in his office, he wanted to know that everyone knew they would be working late tonight and to be ready to start loading quickly, if need be. He was told that Ross would report back to him when Peter and Jones had arrived with the package, then Sonny would run over the plan again when everyone was present.

***

Klass gave up with his phone, he wasn't going to get a signal inside the pub. He'd almost finished his beer; he had nursed it for as long as he could. The noise inside the pub was gradually getting louder with the more alcohol that was being consumed. He stood up and headed towards the bar again, he had to work his way through a large group of people who had been standing drinking since Klass came in. As he approached the bar the same girl with the red Mohican noticed him and asked if he wanted the same again, he nodded and turned to face the front. It was really busy now and almost out of space, he checked his watch, it was 10:35 p.m. and as he looked up, he noticed that there was now a doorman at the entrance, he could see the earpiece in his left ear. An exaggerated cough from the barmaid made him turn back around, he paid for his beer that was sitting in front of him. He picked it up to take a drink and noticed that the door at the end of the corridor was now open, it had been closed earlier, he wasted time checking change in his pocket to try and see if he could see anyone inside, but the angle wasn't great. He was still wary that Jones may appear and recognise him though. He stayed a few minutes then returned to his seat again and waited with one eye on the door.

He didn't have to wait long until Peter appeared in the corridor. Klass pulled his hat down as low as he could just in case, and watched as Peter came out, talking on his mobile phone and walked to the bottom of the dimly lit corridor. He was strangely happy to know that his hunch was justified and following Jones was the right choice, the part that worried him was that he still wasn't able to contact Jane to let her know where he was and even if he could, backup wouldn't get here within the hour. He stuck with his initial instinct and that was to get out the pub. He took one more sip of his beer as he stood and headed towards the entrance, he nodded to the doorman as he left who nodded back before holding the door open for a couple coming in, he slipped past them and out into the crowd.

Peter's phone began ringing twenty minutes after he told Jones not to contact the boss. He answered it but the signal was not great, he was struggling to hear Clarke's instructions on the other side, so he stood up from the table — it wasn't any better, he opened the door into the bar and turned left into the corridor, it wasn't until he walked closer to the backdoor that he could make out what he was saying. After a few minutes talking he went back into the side room again and told Jones to go get the car, they were moving now.

Klass walked slowly across the street from the pub, he was able to blend in pretty well and stopped in a smoking area of a pub that looked into the mouth of the alleyway. He kept an eye on the doorman and at the same time looped around the crowd and managed to enter the alleyway from the other side of the pub. He cautiously crept closer to the backdoor, suddenly a car engine started up and he stood closer to the wall, the headlights pierced the darkness and lit up one half of the opposite wall, he stood motionless as the car turned in the road and reversed up to the fence that surrounded the back door, someone got out and walked round the car and up the step, but he didn't recognise him as it was dark. He continued creeping along to the end of the wall as best he could; he could see exhaust fumes clearly in the cold night air. He peered around the corner, the door was lying open, he checked behind him back up the alleyway, it was still clear, he waited.

***

Ryan's phone lit up again, it was Michael. He told him that he had arranged a car for them, it was parked in a parking lot about three miles from where they were just now, Jane stopped a taxi while Ryan was still on the phone. The driver was talkative, and Ryan had to cut the call to Michael short because he couldn't hear him. It took five minutes to get to the parking lot and Ryan had answered every question from the driver with yes or no and let him rabble on in between. Jane paid and they got out, Michael told them it was a white Audi estate car and the keys would be under the driver side wheel arch. Ryan found the keys and they climbed in, he let Jane drive. It was cold outside — inside the car wasn't much warmer, she started it up and turned the heating up full. She blew into her hands to try and heat them up and looked round at Ryan.

'Where to?' she asked.

***

Klass held his breath as he heard footsteps coming from the rear of the pub, he stood closer to the wall again, he glanced at the car as it sat idling. The first person that came into view was Jones, he had hurried down the stairs and opened the rear door on the driver side before walking back round the car and this time got into the rear passenger seat. A few seconds later a man came down the steps with a hood over his head, followed by Peter — the man Klass had interviewed at the club earlier, who had a hand on the man's shoulder. He led him to the car and lowered his head as he got in, Peter closed the door behind him and went back up the stairs to the pub. Klass exhaled and retreated back into the alleyway, he took out his phone again, he had to call Jane now. He scrolled through his contacts list and found her name, he was just about to press dial when a noise from behind him made him turn around, he froze as the doorman from the pub was walking towards him.

'Hey, what you doing back here?' he asked.

'Sorry, I think I have had a little too much to drink, I stumbled up here thinking I was going to be sick.'

'Well, you can't be sick here; you need to move along!'

'Ok sorry, I will be on my way.' Klass replied and turned back around to see the handle of a gun smashing him on the side of the face. Everything went black as he hit the cold hard ground.

Chapter 32

Klass wasn't knocked out, but he was close to it. The ground was cold against his cheek, he could see blood which had begun to run down his face and over his right eye, he tried to focus, get his bearings, he then tried to prop himself up but couldn't, he wiped the blood from his face instead and looked up to see the figure standing over him, it was Peter. They hadn't noticed him until he had entered the pub, it was the barman cleaning the glasses behind the bar that pointed him out to Peter, he thought he looked and acted strange and when Peter checked the CCTV, he recognised him from the nightclub earlier that day. Klass tried to sit up again but this time Peter pushed him down with his foot.

'That silly bastard Jones should have realised someone might be following him and stopped you coming here, if he had maybe it wouldn't have come to this.' Peter then raised his gun that he had hit him with earlier and pointed it at his face. Klass could make out Jones walking towards him from behind Peters left hand side, as he got closer, he could see a worried look on his face.

'We have to go now; they're waiting on us.' Jones said as he reached peter's side.

Peter never looked round, he instead looked up at the doorman who had been standing there all the time, he nodded to him before turning around and walking back down the alley, then stopped at the entrance to it.

'You said they had moved to plan B didn't you?' Peter said eventually.

Jones didn't know how to respond but he really didn't want this man to be killed.

'He doesn't want any loose ends.' Peter said.

Jones knew what was coming and reached out and grabbed Peters arm, a split second before he pulled the trigger. The bullet missed Klass' head which is where it was aimed, but it did catch him on the side of the neck and almost instantly the blood spurted up and out. Jones pulled at Peters arm again without looking down at Klass, they both turned and walked back to the car. Peter got in the driver's seat next to the man with the hood over his head. The car pulled away slowly, Jones turned in his seat and looked out the rear window and saw the body lying in the alleyway, he turned back around and caught Peters eye in the rear-view mirror looking at him.

'Is that a big enough breadcrumb for you?' Peter said with no expression.

***

Klass was dying, he knew that for sure. He was staring up at the sky with one hand covering the hole in his neck and the other still holding his phone. He had heard the two men walking away after the pop of the gun, he could hear the car being put into gear and pulling away. Loads of things were now going through his mind, most of all was how he had been so stupid and naive, he also knew he had to let Jane know what he found out before he passed out. He used his arm that was still holding the phone to flip himself over onto his front, he didn't have the strength to sit up and the blood from his head and now his neck was in both his eyes. He pressed the phone and it came to life, he tried to find his call list but he was disorientated, and his eyes were thick with blood, he thought he had selected it and pulled the phone closer to him to see but he couldn't tell. He could feel himself slipping away, he hoped it was on her number and he pressed the ok button in the Centre of the phone and prayed it was dialing Jane.

But it never dialed, and Jane's phone never rang. His

arm fell to the floor before he could say anything anyway. The phone hit the ground, just as his last breath left his body.

Chapter 33

Jones waited until they were nearly at the Dutch border before he phoned Michael, to put the next part of the plan into action. Not one of them had spoken the whole way, maybe due to the fact that Peter had just shot an Interpol agent in the neck and left him to die in the alleyway outside a pub in Düsseldorf.

The idea was to now let the agency trace Jones' phone as they made their way to Rotterdam and onto the factory where Sonny would be waiting for them.

Jones dialed Michael's number from his personal phone.

Michael answered his phone but didn't speak.

'Hi Michael, it's Jones.'

'Ok,' he replied.

'I'm just touching base with you to let you know that I'm heading into Amsterdam now, I don't think anything will come from staying in Dortmund. I'm catching the late train to Amsterdam soon and I can meet you in the morning and bring you up to speed. If you can get in touch with Ryan and let him know, he would be as well heading back too.'

'I will pass it on to him, I have to head back to London tonight so it will be just Ryan that can meet you, if he can get back in time. If he does, work closely with him and Jane and bring them up to speed on what's going on.'

'Ok, tell them I will be at central station for 8 a.m.'

Michael ended the call and immediately dialed Ryan.

'Well did he fall for it?' asked Ryan.

'Hard to tell, just carry on like he has,' replied Michael.

'We're heading back to Holland,' he said to Jane when he came off the phone.

Clarke answered on the first ring, as always, Jones had switched back to his burner phone with the one number stored in it.

'We're nearly at the border and we have the package, I've made the call to the agency also. Michael, who is our 2nd in command, is heading back to London tonight. So, if they do pick up on the trace then it should just be Ryan that will be following us to the warehouse, worst case scenario is that the woman is still tagging along with him.'

Clarke hung up the phone.

***

The pickup had passed through the border into Holland with no problems. Clarke had organised for two of Sonny's men to be on duty this week, to make sure that it did, they arrived at the location soon after.

Peter slowed the pick-up and turned onto the road that led down to the warehouse. Production was still in full operation, even at this late hour.

The building itself was massive, it was a rectangular box that covered almost three acres, when it was full, which it had been twice, could hold just under 250,000 tyres. The company sold on average, 6000 tyres per day which were loaded into trucks by an army of warehouse men and delivered mostly in Holland, Germany and France. The deliveries that were made into Britain were usually loaded into steel containers as they were then transported onto container ships. These lorries were loaded from the south side of the building that had eight, forty-foot roller shutter doors that led onto loading bays. The lorries would back up into the building and from there teams of three would lace the tyres into the container. A single container held, on average, 1100 tyres each, depending on the tyre size. This was now far different from when Sonny bought the business twelve years ago and changed it from a major tyre supplier in Holland to a major tyre supplier across Europe. This in turn had made it a very profitable acquisition, and not only as a legitimate business, but it also opened up the possibility for Sonny to export his drugs into new countries all across Europe.

It was when he had set up new customers in Britain to sell tyres too, and therefore needed someone to deal with the logistics, that he was passed the contact information of a university student that had made his name working out how to hide stock and manage the books of a few tyre dealers in Britain. He had contacted this man and had his own men look into him, and when Sonny was happy, he asked him if he could manage the shipment of some of his containers on a pay as you go deal, which he agreed too, and managed very well. After a year of working with Sonny, he asked the man, Clarke, to meet with him in Amsterdam for a meeting regarding a full-time job. Which was rare for Sonny to be so exposed, as he was a fiercely private person, which Clarke later found out. With Clarke's head for business and expertise in logistics and the fact that Britain had now become the company's biggest export for both tyres and drugs, Sonny had offered Clarke a huge advance and yearly salary to be the head of his Operations in Britain, which Clarke happily accepted.

How Sonny managed to smuggle drugs into a handful of different European countries and build his empire was a slightly more difficult endeavor.

The tyre company that he now owned had over fifty heavy goods vehicles and over 100 container boxes. In five of these containers, he had instructed some of his men to design and fabricate a false wall at the front of the container, like a cubby hole. The walls were the full height and length of a standard container, but only 6 inches wide. Which meant that when it was full of cocaine it could hold a street value of 1.2 million euros. The inside of the false wall was lined with a reflective foil that made it difficult, but not impossible, to be detected by the scanners at customs, even with the new advances in technology. The latest scanners that had been designed by the authorities and used in most customs offices around the world had been custom built onto the extending arms of flatbed trucks that were the size of a standard container. The idea behind it was the new scanner was mobile, and therefore can be moved to a particular area to check specific boxes, it could now check twice the number of containers that the old scanners were capable of before. The expanding arm would reach out and the truck would drive through it, the cameras would take a full image of the inside of the container and send the images to a control room, if the control room detected anything suspicious an alarm would sound, and the container would be taken away to be checked manually. If not, it was given a green light to pass through. In the case that something was detected, the container had to be emptied and searched. The disadvantage of this for the customs officers was that a standard container filled with tyres took two and a half hours to unload and a further two and a half to reload, which also had to be done in a specific way to insure the tyres would all fit in. Customs were obviously getting wise to this and so employed ex tyre warehouse workers to do this job for them, but even so with an average of 1000 containers passing through customs each day, to and from Europe, it was impossible to check even 100 of them, which made it very unlikely to be caught. Sonny had also sent only one container filled with drugs every week; he had resisted being too greedy. As an extra precaution he had managed to get a supervisor from customs in Calais on his payroll.

Chapter 34

Michael told Ryan that the phone Jones had used earlier was traceable and they had received a cell ping from a network tower just south of Rotterdam and had managed to pick it up from there. The last update showed the phone being close to an industrial estate in a small town just outside the city. From Google maps they had found out that it was the site of a very large tyre wholesalers, one of the biggest in Holland. Michael passed Ryan the coordinates which he typed into the cars GPS, they were currently on the correct road and would be crossing the border into Holland very soon anyway.

'I think you should try Klass again on the phone, try to feel how he is with you and see if he has been given orders to stop helping us and if you think he still will?' Ryan asked Jane who was concentrating on the road, she hadn't really drove much on the other side of the road and didn't particularly like it, but she didn't want show that in front of Ryan.

'I have left a message, sometimes when he gets caught up in work, he can be hard to get in touch with, he will hopefully phone back soon.'

She drove on for a few miles in silence, thinking about the last few hours and what she may have done that she would need to eventually explain to her bosses.

'I'm not sure I like this Ryan, we have been carrying out our own investigation for nearly a year and a lot of people have spent a lot of time trying to catch this man, and now we can't even be sure if he is still alive.'

She was sounding agitated and unsure. 'And what happens if we are heading straight into a trap here, we don't really know who or what we're dealing with.' She added.

Ryan could understand her worry to a certain point, he

hadn't gotten any further forward in the last 48 hours and as for Sonny there had been no sightings in the media or from the police, he had been dragged out of that café on the Damrak and never seen or heard from again. But Ryan was sure that a lot of the answers could come from Jones, he knew he was involved somehow and was concentrating on finding him first.

'Look I feel the same, let's see what we can find out tonight, and tomorrow we report back to our headquarters and can reassess what to do next.' Ryan said as a way of trying to reassure her.

She nodded, still concentrating on the road.

Chapter 35

In the cold darkness of the alleyway Klass' phone lit up
and beeped. It had done this for the last thirty minutes
from when Jane had left the message and would continue
doing it until the message was listened to or dismissed.

Klass' lifeless body had been lying in the alleyway
since the pickup had drove away earlier. The blood
running from his neck had now turned into a puddle that
had slowly ran into a drain a few feet away. It was on the
fifth beep that a kitchen worker from a restaurant further
up the alley heard it. The man was standing at the fire
exit to the kitchen smoking a cigarette on his break, when
he thought he could hear a noise, he took a step out of the
doorway and looked down. The alleyway was badly lit,
and he couldn't see anyone standing in it. He took a step
back but again he heard the noise a few seconds later, he
stepped out this time and started walking towards where
he thought it was coming from, it wasn't until he was
nearly standing on top of the phone that he saw the man's
body lying on the ground with a hole in the side of his
neck. He dropped his cigarette and raced back to the
kitchen and called for the police.

***

Peter parked the car close to a side entrance and all three
men got out, Peter leading the man with the bag over his
head, first. Jones then got in the driver's seat and parked
the car round the back of the warehouse building, out of
sight of the main entrance. Once they had locked the
package away, they headed for Sonny's office. Sonny and
Clarke were both sitting behind desks, Ross the
warehouse operations manager was standing in the corner
next to an older man who was wearing suit trousers and

had spiked hair that was wet with gel. The office was huge and spotlessly clean, there was massive screens on two of the walls, one had 9 CCTV channels running and the other was showing a repeat of a Dutch football match.

When everyone was in Sonny's office and listening, he ran through the plan, the new plan. Everyone there except for Jones was aware that he had sold the tyre company and the new owners were taking over in less than a week. All of the workers involved in the company, as well as Peter and Clarke, had been well compensated and most of them were keeping their jobs, which Sonny had made sure off in the negotiating of the business.

He started by running through what had already been done, mostly by Ross his operations manager and his workers. So far, they had already loaded three containers full of tyres, and had a full staff working through the night to help load another two, and to protect Sonny if need be. As soon as Ryan arrived, he was to be lured into the building where, if all went well, he would be apprehended and held with the package Peter and Jones had brought in earlier. From there Sonny made it clear that he had to physically be there to see both these men killed before he could begin to make his escape. Once this part of the plan was executed, the next step would be even more complicated.

Sonny was then to be loaded into the back of one of his containers. He had adapted one specifically in the same way that he had to smuggle the drugs but this time, with a gap in between of two feet instead of six inches, which was just big enough for him to lie out flat. The fake wall was lined with the same material that helped prevent it from showing the drugs on the scanner at customs, if the container was stopped that was. Again, with his man on the inside that Peter had already paid off, he was hoping that it wouldn't be. Inside he had thermal blankets, water and a few snacks and enough holes drilled into the side walls to make sure he could breathe.

Sonny then made sure that there were enough workers across the warehouse who were armed, which Ross assured him there was, and that if it came to it, he had five men that would be able to load the container full of tyres in fifty-five minutes. He was glad to hear that and told him to make sure everyone was alert, and that Ryan could be here soon.

Chapter 36

The air was cold, a freezing fog was hovering over the warehouse as the white Audi approached the entrance road. Jane turned off the headlights and pulled the car over to the side. The building itself was huge, it was 300 hundred yards down the road from where they were sitting. It sat alone surrounded by a perimeter fence and beyond that, trees for as far as they could see. The warehouse was still busy, even at this hour, there was HGV'S driving back and forth from one door to another, they could also see dozens of men in protective jackets walking in and out the shutter doors, which would make getting close difficult. That wasn't including the fact that the whole place was so brightly lit up, you could see it for miles, if not for the fog floating above.

They were fairly sure that the front gates would have security cameras covering it and possibly the road leading to it, but they had no choice but to drive down. Jane put the car into gear and the large tyres crunched on the patches of ice that had started to form on the uneven road. She drove slowly, keeping watch for someone coming to meet them or making their way over to the booth that sat between the two front gates, but no one did. Jane turned the car and stopped in front of the left-hand gate, the booth was empty, and the security barrier was down, they looked at each other. Jane was just about to speak when the barrier suddenly lifted, neither of them thought it would work off a sensor, so someone must know that they were there. Jane crept forward and drove slowly into the car park. She parked the car on the left-hand side of the huge parking area that looked across to the entrance of the warehouse. They sat there unsure of how to proceed, they never thought they would have gotten this far with no resistance. Jones phone had been traced to this location, but the location as it turned out was huge, and finding him could still be tricky.

***

Sonny and Clarke were still in Sonny's office when the call came through from his reception.

'Hey boss, we just picked up a white Audi estate car, it stopped at the top of the road for a few minutes then moved down to the front gates, it's sitting there now.'

'Hang on.' Sonny replied and clicked his computer to life, he scrolled down and opened the feed of the CCTV cameras. 'Ok I got it, keep an eye on them just now and keep me on loudspeaker.'

Sonny selected the camera that looked onto the front gates that was mounted onto the booth in the middle, he turned it to face the car side on and zoomed in as close as he could get it. The windows were tinted — he couldn't make out any details of who were inside.

'Is that them?' Sonny said to Clarke pointing at the screen, he had slid his chair up next to Sonny's.

'I think so,' he replied. 'There is definitely two of them in the car and it looks like the woman from Interpol driving.'

'Can't we get a better camera angle?' Sonny said into the phone.

'Sorry boss, it's the best angle we got, it's too dark to see inside.'

He thought for a few seconds then spoke again.

'Lift the barrier and make sure everyone is ready,' he said and hung up the phone.

Not everyone that worked in the company was aware of who owned the business and what their biggest source of income was, that would be far too risky. The man who noticed the white Audi was named Jaap and he was now approaching the car, he was one of the workers who wasn't aware. He was a dispatch supervisor who had noticed the car at the barrier before eventually coming in. He headed over to see if he could help them, he said hello in Dutch and when Jane replied in English he quickly switched.

'Hi, is there anything I can help you with?' the man's English wasn't too bad and they could understand him ok.

'Yes, thanks,' Jane replied through the gap she made by buzzing the window down. 'We are looking to speak to whoever is in charge please, we're from compliance.'

The man hesitated trying to understand. 'Ok, I will get someone for you,' he headed back towards the building.

'I say we give it five minutes and if nobody comes out, we head for the reception.'

'Ok,' replied Jane. 'I hope this works.'

***

As soon as he disappeared through the shutter, he was called on by one of the workers in the warehouse, he was told to go upstairs, the boss wanted to see him. He huffed and headed up the stairs to the offices.

He knocked on the door and was shouted in. Sonny was sitting behind his desk looking annoyed, the slim English man who had been spending more time here recently was sitting next to him. There was also one of the managers standing against a filing cabinet in the corner, he thought his name was Peter.

'Sit down Jaap.' Sonny said and pointed to the chair on the other side of his desk. 'What's going on with the white Audi in the car park?' Sonny asked him.

'I noticed it coming in but never recognised it, and when no one got out I thought I would go and see who it was.'

'And?'

'It was a man and a woman, they said that they were from compliance and wanted to speak to whoever is in charge.' Jaap answered.

'What did you say?'

'I said I would find someone to speak with them.'

'You get their names?'

'No, sorry.'

'Ok, you can head back down, good job.'

Jaap got up and headed out of the office, Peter started talking when he closed the door.

'They are aware, I would assume, that no one is going to go out there and they might be stalling for time, maybe waiting for back up.'

'I don't think so,' said Clarke. 'If they were waiting for backup they would have waited around the corner and all come in together.'

'You sure?' said Peter.

'We have to assume that they have found the body in Düsseldorf but I doubt they would have identified him this early, and as we know there is no way of getting any CCTV footage from the alleyway so I would guess they have picked up the trace on Jones' phone as we had planned and that's it. They will have no idea they are walking into a trap and that any of us are here.'

'What do we do next then?' Sonny asked.

'If we do nothing, they will have to make their way inside and that's what we wanted anyway, maybe not this quick and without having the woman from Interpol tagging along, but if we wait on them getting inside and hold them, we can carry on with the plan.'

'Ok, we wait.' said Sonny.

Chapter 37

The Düsseldorf police arrived shortly after receiving a call from the worker in the restaurant. Three squad cars had been dispatched and were all on the scene when the lead detective arrived, both ends of the alleyway had been cordoned off and the pub and restaurants were told to close their side doors onto the alleyway. The body had been covered with a tent to protect any evidence while the forensics team were setting up.

The lead detective was Oliver Stam. He had been a police officer for eighteen years and a detective for twelve and according to his fellow detectives he gave the impression that he didn't particularly enjoy his job, which wasn't true, it was just the way he came across to some people. He was divorced with a daughter who was currently two years into a six-month trip across Thailand.

Oliver was the first person to examine the body and could clearly see the gunshot wound on the dead man's neck and the blood that had flowed from it, which was now starting to congeal on the icy pavement. He called on one of the uniformed officers to bring him up to speed on what had been done so far. The officer told him that the kitchen worker from a Chinese restaurant further up the alleyway who discovered the body hadn't seen or heard anything, it was only when he was on his break and came out into the alleyway for a cigarette that he thought he heard a beeping noise. He headed down the alleyway and found the body before running back and calling the police.

Oliver had a look up at where he was told the worker came out from and then back down at the rear of the pub where the man was lying. 'Ok, where are we now?'

'My colleague is in the pub just now, he told the doorman to lock it up and not to let anyone leave, including the staff, until a detective arrived.'

'That's good,' said Oliver. 'We can start questioning everyone inside and taking names and addresses, I want to check for CCTV,' and pointed towards a camera at the rear of the pub, 'we might get lucky.'

The officer nodded and they headed for the front of the pub.

***

After five minutes, the man Jane had spoken with hadn't come back and neither did anyone else, so they decided to head for the reception.

They got out the car into the bitter cold and pulled their hats down as much as they could to keep their heads warm. The car park had been gritted which helped as they walked slowly down a slope towards the front door. Jane pulled open one of the doors and they headed into the welcomed heat of what was a very modern reception area. It was filled with grey and white, both the décor and furniture. There was a coffee machine in the corner and at least four large television screens mounted on walls, one of them had the local news channel on and the rest were displaying adverts for various tyre manufacturers.

A small mousey looking woman with glasses that were too big for her face was sitting behind the reception, she smiled at them as they came in. She had just hung up on a call from her boss Sonny telling her to let the two people who were on their way in to take a seat, and someone would be with them soon.

'Hi, were here to speak with the owner or person in charge please.'

'Certainly, we have been expecting you, please take a seat and someone will be right down.'

She gestured towards a door at the other end of the

reception which led to a waiting room that was designed better than most people's living rooms. It had a large expensive table in the middle and was scattered with designer looking chairs and stools. They sat as far from the reception as possible but didn't speak, Jane felt a little nervous which was unusual for her in these situations, her right leg began to shake. She rested her hands on it to stop it, she had just about managed to when one of the double doors opened and a tall man with broad shoulders and blond hair came through.

'My name is Carl, could you follow me please,' he said in a cheery voice.

Sonny watched from the screen on his desk as both of them entered the reception and took a seat in the waiting room, he agreed with Clarke that they must not have any clue what they were heading in to. He then spoke with Clarke and agreed that he didn't want any chance of them bumping into Jones or Peter who they would recognise, and he certainly didn't want anyone knowing that the package was locked up here also. He buzzed down to Carl and told him to go get them and take them to meeting room A. From there they could be contained and held for Sonny to deal with.

***

Most of the officers were on patrol duty, telling curious passersby to keep on moving. Oliver had caught up with the officer that had gone into the pub to make enquiries, he had taken a quick statement from almost half of the patrons and most of them said roughly the same thing, they didn't see anyone suspicious, and they didn't hear any gunshot because of the music that was playing. A few were too drunk and still weren't aware what had happened, and another said he could phone a guy who would tell the police who done it for forty euros and some weed.

Oliver then made his way through the back, the barmaid who was working behind the bar at the time was waiting to be interviewed by him, Oliver thought her hair was pretty cool.

They both took a seat in a back office facing onto the bar, Oliver was trying not give away too much to see what she knew first.

'As you may know by now a man has been found dead in the alleyway running alongside the bar outside, are you aware of any disturbances or altercations inside the bar tonight.'

The woman spoke like a stroppy teenager who would rather be anywhere else than sitting here talking to the police.

'No, it's been busy tonight but uneventful,' she replied.

'My assistant has told me that you have CCTV on the inside of the bar but not on the outside, even though there is a camera mounted on the wall, why is that?'

'It was broken a few months back.'

'Why didn't you get it fixed?'

'No idea, it's not my pub, I just work here,' she replied looking straight through him.

'Ok can you tell me who does own it then?' He asked a little annoyed.

The woman swung back in her chair.

'I don't know who owns the place but the guy who pays my wages is called Peter, he stops by once a week to pay us and make sure everything is ok.'

'What's his second name?'

The woman shrugged; she wasn't going to help anyone tonight.

Oliver got up to leave and had to fight the urge of

nudging the chair she was swinging on and watching her fall back on her ass. Just as the urge passed, his assistant who had been scanning through the CCTV footage of the bar came in.

'I think we got something' he said.

'Stay here,' he said to the woman.

The footage wasn't great because of the lighting in the bar. The tape was paused at 10:34 p.m. he could see the back of a red Mohican on the screen, the camera looked onto the till from the bar side.

'So, what you got?' said Oliver.

The screen jumped to life, and you could see a man approaching the bar and speak to the woman, he had his jacket zipped up tight to his face and a hat on his head, when the woman moved away to presumably pour his drink you could clearly see that it was the same man from the alleyway outside. They paused the screen again and Oliver walked back and asked the woman to come out and join them.

She came through and looked at the screen.

'Is that the guy?' she asked.

'Yes, do you recognise him?' Oliver asked her.

'Yes,' she looked closer at the screen. 'He sat alone in the left-hand side of the bar and had two beers, one after the other.'

'Did he ask anything strange or act strange?'

'He only asked for his drink both times, I remember him because he kept his hat and jacket on.'

Oliver asked for the footage to be forwarded onto him, he then thanked the woman and told her the pub was now closed for tonight which she didn't seem too bothered by. He headed out of the pub and turned up the alleyway, he had a quick look for cameras facing the alleyway but found none. As he walked by the cordon, he saw that the forensics team had begun examining the body, as he approached one of them spotted him and told him they would be finished in a few minutes. Oliver nodded and took out a cigarette and lit it up, he took a draw and blew out the smoke and watched as it circled upwards into the sky above.

Chapter 38

Carl held the door open for them as they stood up and walked towards him, he was at least 6 feet 3 inches, he closed the door behind them as they went through.

'Take a left up ahead then it's the first door on the right.' Carl said.

Jane turned around and looked back nervously. The halls were long and the same colour as the reception, both the walls and floor. She could hear the buzz of a working environment, the sound of chatter and the noise from the engines starting up and moving, it had a weird smell too, like burning rubber.

They took the first left and could see the first door on the right, it was the only door that was on the right. As they got close to it, they could see inside through a large glass window, it was a meeting or conference room. It had a large rectangular table that took up most of the room and was surrounded by chairs, there was a projector on one wall and a whiteboard on the other, Jane hesitated at the door.

'Go ahead, take a seat and the boss will be down shortly.'

Carl smiled at them and closed the door over.

The room was warm and everything else looked as it did from the outside, except for the window next to the door, it wasn't a window on the inside, it was only one way, all they could see when they looked out was a reflection of themselves.

'I don't like this,' said Jane.

'Me neither.'

After locking the meeting room door over Carl made his way to Sonny's office, he knocked before entering.

'Are they in, ok?' Sonny asked.

'Yeah boss, no resistance, they just walked straight in

and sat down. I told them to wait, and I would come and get you.'

Sonny turned to Clarke. 'Something doesn't seem right; they can't be that naive.'

'I told you earlier, they must have no clue what this place is or who owns it.' Clarke replied.

'Do you think they're armed?' Sonny asked Carl.

'I couldn't tell but I would expect them both to be.'

'Ok, let's do this now, get another one of your guys and we will all go in, a bullet in each of them and then head to the hold room and finish this.'

'Ok boss.' He headed to the door and radioed for one of his men to head for meeting room A.

Chapter 39

The head forensic officer took off one of her gloves and wiped her forehead, she looked round for Oliver, they had met a few times previously at other crime scenes. She spotted him standing further down the alleyway smoking a cigarette, she shouted on him — he turned to see who it was, she waved him over, he took a last draw from his cigarette and through the butt on the ground and headed over.

They shook hands when he got to her.

'As you will have worked out yourself, he has a gunshot wound on the left-hand side of his neck, this is the cause of death, the bullet had gone through and out the other side, we managed to recover it and it's being sent away for testing. There is also a bad cut on the back of his head which we think is from a blunt object and must have been done with a lot of force. I'm also pretty sure he didn't die instantly, there seems to be two pools of blood which would suggest movement after being shot, there is so much blood that we think the heart was still pumping it when he moved.

Oliver looked down at the body and then back up at the officer.

'That seems strange, could he have been moved?'

'We can't see any grab marks on him or see any other blood marks, so we don't think so.'

Oliver tried to work out what could have happened.

'We're going to get packed up now, the coroner is on their way.'

She handed Oliver a plastic bag that had a few of the man's possessions in it that had been recovered from the scene.

'We also found a mobile phone close to the man's right hand that had quite a bit of blood on it, so we're sending it for testing too, we will contact you when we are done, and you can come and collect it.'

Inside the bag was some loose change, a few notes, and a wallet. Oliver took out the wallet, it was real brown leather, well used. He looked through it to try and find some identification for the man, he saw from his driving license that the man's name was Klass, he took it out and kept looking. There was some store cards and a bank card, he took them out and another card that was behind them fell out, he picked it up and checked it.

'Shit' he said out loud and took his phone from his inside pocket and dialed his station. He got put through to his sergeant. 'Oliver, what we got?'

'The body in the alleyway that I got assigned too.'

'Yes, how you getting on?'

'Forensics just passed me his belongings and I got his identification from his wallet.'

'And?'

'He's an Interpol agent.'

'Shit,' the sergeant said as well and hung up so he could phone his boss.

***

Sonny and Clarke followed behind the two security men as they walked up the corridor to the meeting room, no one spoke.

Sonny let himself think for a second of how close he was to pulling this off and making his way back to Britain and hopefully to his family; it had been fourteen years since they had all been together. Sonny had got them new identities and moved them away from where they originally lived, they were looked after financially and had everything they ever wanted but now he wanted to be a part of it again.

This wasn't the only reason for him wanting to return home, the way he had lived for the past ten years had meant he had made a lot of enemies and he was clever enough to know that the authorities would be closing in on him, buying the tyre company had exposed him but he needed it to clean as much of the drug money as he could.

Another big part of getting out was that in the past year, Romanians had moved in on Amsterdam and began fighting for some of Sonny's territories, Sonny had lost three men in the last two months alone from clashes with them and he knew it would only escalate if he retaliated.

As they approached the door of the meeting room the two security men took out their guns, they still didn't expect any resistance, but they were taking no chances. Sonny stopped and looked through the mirrored window first as Clarke followed behind him, he could see them both sitting at the table that faced the window, knowing they couldn't see him.

'I still can't believe they walked straight in here,' he said to Clarke who was now standing next to him looking through the window as well. The woman looked a little nervous and appeared to be staring straight at Sonny.

'I know, we always thought this would be the difficult part of the plan.'

Through the window they saw the woman saying something, but they couldn't hear what it was from outside. After a few seconds the man inside pulled his hands back and rested them on his lap and sat back in his chair, he lifted his head and looked out the window.

'Ok, let's go in and get this over with.' Sonny said to his security men, but they were interrupted by Clarke.

'What the hell!' he had said loudly.

'What is it?' said Sonny annoyed.

'That man in there isn't Ryan!'

Ryan had been running for nearly twenty minutes and physically, he was feeling it. He had got out of the Audi a few miles away from the location that the trace on Jones' phone had given them, he got off the main road and made his way down a dirt track for a mile until he saw the bright lights of the warehouse, this gave him the chance to try and get his bearings. He figured he was at the corner of the building that led down to the front entrance and realised he wanted to be at the opposite corner to that, so he cut off the dirt track and into the trees which surrounded the whole building. He was careful as he ran through, the ground was solid and dense with lots of roots and loose branches that he couldn't see very well in the dark.

He kept a steady pace until he reached the first corner, he stopped and put his hands on his knees, he tried to catch his breath, but it was hard in the cold night air. When he knew the rear of the building was clear he let himself get a bit closer to the surrounding fence and ran along the top side of the building. He stopped before reaching the far end and looked down at the first of the loading bays. There were plenty of heavy good vehicles inside, some loading, some unloading and some sitting waiting to be guided into the bays. From what he could see there wasn't any cameras that looked onto the back fence where he hoped to get access from. If he managed to get over the fence and into the warehouse, he would try and blend in with the workers.

He took out a pair of gloves from his coat pocket and put them on and pulled his hat down over his ears, he reached up and pulled himself upwards onto the fence and jumped over, he landed with a thud and looked up at the huge warehouse in front of him, so far so good.

Chapter 41

Michael, not Ryan after all, looked round again at Jane and smiled.

'Well, I'm pretty sure they know who I am now, or who I am not, so be prepared.'

Ryan and Jane had picked Michael up ten minutes after crossing the border into Holland, he had borrowed a car from the agency and drove to a small town that was on the same route Ryan and Jane would be passing through. After the usual pleasantries Michael brought them up to speed on what he had found out since speaking to Ryan last, which turned out to be quite a lot.

It took most of the journey for Michael to explain everything.

Not long after coming off the phone to Ryan earlier he received a call from another one of the agencies intelligence directors that he had come up through the ranks with, starting from their field agent days during the Cold War. As Michael had been informed earlier, not long after his meeting with Ryan at the football match there had been a special unit deployed to search for the director General who had went missing. That's when the boss had been last spotted, and as it turned out, was in Amsterdam city centre, he had been seen departing a train in central station just after 9 a.m. three days ago, the day of the meeting at the café. The special unit had located CCTV of him coming out of the station and disappearing not long after, no further sightings had been reported and no more information had been found regarding him until yesterday evening.

On the outskirts of the city centre a tourist had been recording one of the many canal boats coming into the city, the video was nearly fifteen minutes long and it wasn't until yesterday when that man returned home to

Sweden and looked through all of his photos and videos that he spotted the scene.

About ten minutes into the clip, he captures what looks like an ordinary white van pulling up to the curb 20 yards down the street, the camera is focusing on a boat on the canal that is moving slowly. As the tourist is following the boat, on the left of the screen a tall man with black hair and a long black jacket comes into view, the image is not great but it's visible. Just as the tourist is about to move again, putting the van out of shot, the driver's door opens, someone steps out and stands in front of the man with the black coat, we assume an exchange of words takes place and after what seems like a split second the man is grabbed from behind and thrown into what must be the side door of the van. The man who grabs him isn't visible up until then, he must have come out the passenger side and around the back of the van, the driver then quickly turns and jumps into the driver's seat and the van pulls away.

Ryan had asked if any of the men were identified but Michael explained that the focus of the camera had been on the canal boat which makes the quality of the images of the men poor. The one thing being positive was when they enhanced and zoomed in on the van, they managed to get the license plate from it, and it had come back to a small accounting firm in Brussels. Ryan and Jane looked across at each other when Michael told them this. '*As we looked into this it came up in our records that two previous license numbers that you had checked regarding this case had also come back the same, so naturally we got our guys to look further into it and a special team has been finding all they can on this small accounting firm in Brussels. After hours of digging, they realised that the business is a front which has an address of a small café in Brussels, but the bank accounts are legitimate. This is when they contacted me as one of the accounts has links with a very large tyre wholesaler in Holland and funnily enough the postcode is the same as the trace we have on Jones' phone.'*

Both Ryan and Jane looked into the back of the car at Michael. He told them that they were now sure that this all had to be connected somehow, it was far too much of a coincidence. His boss then told Michael to meet up with Ryan and Jane and try to get access to the warehouse and come up with a plan on how to do so. After half an hour discussing, and a few ideas, Ryan had come up with the idea of Michael and Jane walking into the building with Michael trying to conceal his identity. Jane saw the resemblance between Ryan and Michael as soon as she saw him and thought that he could maybe pass as him too, that way Ryan could then try and enter the building undetected and hopefully find Jones or at least get some intel on what was going on inside.

Chapter 42

Jane and Michael heard the click of the door handle before they saw it open, they kicked their legs back and their chair's slammed against the wall behind them, the two security men were both armed and aiming their guns at them as they rushed in, the second guy was shorter than the one that had brought them to the meeting room, he had his gun pointed at Michael's chest. Sonny and Clarke had already made their way back to Sonny's office.

'Both of you turn around and face the wall, now!'

'What's going on?' Michael said calmly considering the gun pointed at him.

'You know what's going on, shut up and face the wall.'

The shorter of the men kept his gun pointed at them as Carl frisked them both, he didn't find a gun on Jane and took Michael's handgun from his belt holder, he then cable tied them both and slumped them down against the wall.

'I'm going to speak to the boss, if any of them move, shoot the other one.' Carl said before leaving the room and shutting the door over. The shorter guy nodded.

Clarke was fixed on the CCTV screen when Carl came into the office, Sonny was sitting next to him and looked a little anxious as he watched.

'Everything ok?' he asked Carl.

'They didn't put up a fight, I have cable tied their hands and feet and one of the guys is watching over them, only the man was armed as well, we took a handgun from him, what's the plan now?'

Clarke never looked away from the screen when he spoke. 'It's got to be a decoy, they must have planned for us not recognising him as Ryan, so he has to be trying to get in some other way without being detected,' he said to no one in particular.

'He is getting the upper hand,' said Sonny.

'I still don't think that they know who we have inside the building, and I believe it's still just the two in the meeting room and Ryan that's looking into us, and we know that Interpol have stopped assisting the woman.' Clarke said.

'We still go ahead with the plan, we kill everyone, Ryan will have to turn up sooner or later and we deal with him then.' Sonny spoke knowing that if for some reason he got away in the container and never managed to kill Ryan he would always be watching his back, he hoped he would be caught before he had to leave.

'Carl, we will deal with the man we have in the hold room and the two in the meeting room, I need you to get all of your men together and hunt Ryan down, he has to be found.'

'Ok boss.' Carl said and turned to leave just as Clarke said,

'I think I found him.'

Chapter 43

Ryan kept as close to the outer fence as he could to avoid being detected, he had 20 yards until he reached the corner of the building. He peered around it, the first of the loading bays was another 20 yards down again, he knew he could get there in a matter of seconds, but he also knew he would be easier to spot if he started running. He noticed three cameras mounted on the inside of the outer fence and knew at least two of them would capture his next movements. He waited a few seconds then turned the corner and walked briskly along the front of the building. As he reached the first bay a driver who had just backed his vehicle in, jumped down from his cab, he saw Ryan and said something to him in Dutch that Ryan never understood, he replied hello anyway.

The driver took the steps up to the loading bay that were bolted onto the side of the concrete bay and disappeared. Ryan took the opportunity to open his driver's door, he stood on the top step and leaned in. Inside he found a reflective jacket and a hard hat lying behind the passenger's seat, he jumped back down and put them both on and headed up the same steps as the driver and made his way into the warehouse.

***

Sonny had wasted no more time when he was positive that the man who had jumped the back fence and walked down the side of the building was Ryan, he had to leave now.

He told Clarke to take a handgun from the safe that was built into his office wall, hidden behind a tired looking painting. He then instructed Carl and his team to catch Ryan and kill him at once, he was going to head for the container. The plan had changed again.

'Clarke, head down to the hold room, Peter is in there with Jones, tell him that I'm leaving now and to do as me and him discussed earlier today, and remember, no loose ends.'

'Ok.' Clarke said as he put the handgun, he took from the safe on the wall in his coat pocket and walked over to Sonny who had stood up from his desk. 'See you on the other side boss,' he said and shook Sonny's hand.

Carl checked the hallway outside Sonny's office door, in both directions before telling Sonny to follow closely. Carl was now going to make sure that Sonny got to the container safely before returning to take care of the two that were being held in the meeting room, whoever they were. They ran down the hallway and passed the meeting room, Carl had a quick look in on the way past and saw that Jane and Michael were still tied and sitting on the floor against the wall. They then took a right turn which led onto a fire exit, Carl pushed on the bar at the front which opened with a bang into another huge warehouse, it was a mirror image of the loading bay on the other side, where containers were loaded from, it looked even bigger as it was almost empty. Halfway down the warehouse were five containers sitting side by side, four of them were locked up and waiting, drivers in their cab and the fifth container, the one in the middle, had six men standing at the back of it, surrounded by twenty large cages that were on wheels, they were full of tyres — at least fifty in each. One of the men was the operations manager Ross, he told his workers to look sharp when they saw that it was Sonny that was running down the warehouse. Sonny never said anything to the men as he got to the container, he just headed inside, followed by Ross who gave him a bag with his supplies. Sonny thanked him and pulled on his thermal clothing and slid in through the false wall which Ross closed over after him. It was freezing inside, like a portable icebox, sonny slipped into his sleeping bag that was also thermal, he lay down and pulled his Eskimo hat over his head, he knew this was going to be a long two days.

After securing the false door at the back of the container, Ross walked back out and told his guys to go as fast as they could, they had one thousand tyres to load. Two men went inside the container, who would lace the tyres in a specific way that allowed them to get more in. The two men on the outside would roll the tyres into them, the fifth guy just helped when needed. Ross told them they had fifty minutes, if they could do it in forty-five, they could get the rest of the week off.

Chapter 44

Clarke followed Carl and Sonny out of Sonny's office but he turned right instead of left. He hurried down the hallway as fast as he could. The hold room was at the other end of the hallway from Sonny's office, and it only took him a minute to get there, he entered and closed the door behind him, quickly but quietly.

The room was about the same size as Sonny's office but with a different layout. All that was in it was a large table in the middle with six chairs surrounding it, there was a desk chair against the back wall and a counter with a kettle and toaster on it. A large TV was hung on the wall, but it was turned off.

Peter was standing at the counter when Clarke came in, his gun and cigarettes were sitting on the table in the middle of the room. The man with the hood over his head was sitting at the head of the table. Jones was sitting at the desk with his laptop open, Peter looked round as soon as he heard the door.

'What's going on out there?' he asked.

'The man and woman that we have been expecting just entered through reception, they walked in themselves, no hesitation.'

'So, we got them, we can end this shit tonight?' Peter asked.

'Not quite, we took them to the meeting room and locked them in, but as we returned with Sonny so he could kill them, Clarke saw the man's face and told us that he wasn't Ryan.'

Peter looked confused, 'who the hell is he then?'

'We don't know.'

'Where is Ryan?'

'In here somewhere, we think, we spotted him on CCTV ten minutes ago jumping over the back fence at the far end of the warehouse.'

Peter lifted his gun from the table.

'I will check and see if I recognise the man in the meeting room, then I'm going to do what I should have done at the start of all this and kill Ryan myself.'

'Wait!' Clarke shouted just before he left. 'Sonny is already being loaded into the container to escape, he told me to remind you about what you both spoke about earlier today, there has to be no loose ends.'

At the sound of Sonny's name, the man in the hood reacted, slightly. Not enough for Clarke, or Peter to notice, but that was the first time that he had actually heard his name being used. Peter looked back at the man who was still sitting at the table and then over at Jones who was watching them but hadn't said anything yet. 'I will be back in ten. Make sure no one leaves this room.'

Chapter 45

Jane hated being restrained, her hands and feet were tied tight, and she couldn't move either of them, not even an inch. The one thing she was happy about was that the blonde security guy hadn't searched her very well, he had found and took Michael's gun from him but he hadn't checked her ankle holder where she kept a small handgun, the only problem was getting a hand free to use it. They also never took away her mobile phone, I'm assuming they didn't think it would be much use with their hands being tied up or more worryingly if they were going to end up dead soon anyway. She just had to trust Ryan with what they had planned and hopefully he was already in the building and closing in on Jones, if Jones was still here that was.

***

Ryan had walked past two loading bays before turning in through one of the huge shutter doors into the main warehouse. The smell of rubber was so strong, the inside of the warehouse looked even bigger than it did from the outside, it was filled from wall to wall with tyres of all different makes and sizes, they all had different shiny labels on them that were facing out so they could be identified by make and size, he assumed.

It looked like it was at peak time for the warehouse, there were teams of workers spread all over the place. Far into the warehouse Ryan could see men on forklifts, they were lifting blue stillages that were full of tyres and stacked five high, they would move them into specific loading areas that were marked on the concrete floor with paint, words wrote in Dutch that Ryan couldn't understand. From here the tyres would then be either rolled directly into the back of the container or placed onto a rack that had four levels to it, the men at the opposite side of the rack would then lift the tyres and load them into the containers, there was a worker standing at the edge of every container who was also checking every tyre that went inside.

Ryan stood watching the process for a minute before trying to locate some kind of office or staff room where he could hopefully get information on Jones. He noticed that all the people who worked in the warehouse or for the company as a driver, wore the same uniform, a dark red T-shirt with the company's logo on the front, he could also make out that a lot of the drivers didn't have any uniform on, he hoped no one would notice him without one on either. After looking around for a bit he found a door on the far side of the warehouse that had a constant stream of workers coming in and out of it. He kept his head low and made his way towards it.

Inside was what he would describe as a large waiting room/canteen, there was half a dozen benches placed at one end where a few workers were eating lunch. They looked more like drivers rather than warehouse staff, the majority of them were drinking coffee from plastic cups from a coffee machine that sat in the far corner. At the opposite side of the room to Ryan was a long counter, like a parts counter. There was two women and a man working on the other side, all three had the company shirt on. Ryan made his way across to the coffee machine and took out a Euro, he pressed the button for a white americano and tipped some sugar into the cup, the machine whizzed and gurgled before the water poured out. He lifted it and stirred the sugar in and had a closer look at the counter.

The coffee tasted terrible, but it gave him some time to figure out what was going on. From what he could make out, all the containers and tyres that were coming in or going out of the warehouse had to pass through here first. All the paperwork would be checked, stamped and the driver given a time to be loaded or unloaded and from what loading bay this would be done. The driver would park up in the car park and bring his paperwork in here, he would then hitch or unhitch his load, loading was on the west side of the building and unloading on the east side. The driver would then either stay in his cab and eat or sleep or head into this canteen to catch up with other drivers. Ryan knew he had no paperwork, but he had to get beyond that counter. He took a chance and headed over to the friendliest looking of the two women.

'Hi, I'm looking for some help,' Ryan said to her.

The woman smiled back without saying anything.

'I was here just over a month ago and handed in a CV, I was told to let someone know the next time I was delivering here so I could arrange an interview. Can you see if this would be possible today, please?'

The woman smiled back as if happy to be asked anything other than just containers.

'Wait here,' she replied and disappeared through the back.

For a moment Ryan thought that he could have made a grave mistake, but after a short time the woman reappeared.

'Helen deals with recruitment but she is on her break at the moment, she is due back in ten minutes. If you want to wait, go back out the door and take a left, her office is the next one along.'

Ryan thanked the woman and followed her directions; he opened the door he was told to which led him into a waiting room that had three smaller offices attached. There were only three chairs in the waiting room, he sat in the one in the middle, and waited.

Peter had his gun in his hand and his hand by his side as he hurried up the hallway. He was annoyed at not being given the go ahead to kill Ryan back in Amsterdam and now look at what it had come to. He reached the meeting room and pushed the door open, he looked at Jane and then at Michael and realised he was the man he had saw speaking with Ryan at the stadium. They were still tied up and slouched in a half sitting, half lying position on the floor. One of Carl's security men was standing by them with his gun pointed at them both.

'Where the hell is he?' Peter shouted.

'You tell us, if I was you though I would watch your back, he will be coming soon.' Jane replied.

Peter smirked. 'I'm the one holding the gun here sweetheart, and it looks to me like you should have stuck to your day job and not tried to be the hero.'

Jane smiled back.

'I've already killed one of you lot recently and I don't plan on stopping with him.'

Jane thought about Klass' man from the nightclub, it must have been him who done it. She got angry but never let it show.

'I'm going to look for Ryan, if anyone of them moves or says anything, shoot the other one in the head.'

The security man nodded as Peter left. Peter then made his way to the reception where he could check the CCTV for himself and see where Ryan had gained access.

***

Ryan stood up when he thought the woman that came in was Helen, as it turned out the woman was called Anne and worked in accounts.

Ryan had realised while waiting that his interview story wasn't that great and no way could he sit for an interview anyway, so at the last minute he had a change of plan.

'Hi, I have been sent in to check your heating system, the lady from the counter told me to speak to someone in here, she said you could let me through.'

'Ok,' the woman hesitated, 'I didn't know we had a problem?' she replied.

'Hopefully there won't be, I'm just here to service it today.'

Ryan knew if this never worked, he had no time to waste and would have to barge through the door into the offices behind and blow his cover, which he really did not want to do. After a brief phone call the woman opened the sliding glass window.

'That's fine, come through, I've buzzed the door open for you.'

'Thanks.' Ryan said as he headed for the door.

The woman took him to the service room that the boiler for the main offices was in and asked him if she could leave him on his own to get on with it, he smiled and said sure. After she had left, Ryan left the room and came out into the corridor. The floor was tiled in grey and the walls painted white, the floor was slippery under his feet. He had no way of knowing where he was heading, he cautiously kept walking up the corridor until he reached the double doors that led to the reception, he walked through and stopped as the receptionist who was sitting at her desk looked up at him.

'Can I help you?' she asked a little bemused.

'Yes, I'm here about a job and have been sent to speak to the owner but I can't find his office.' He changed his story again.

The woman told Ryan to carry on further up the corridor and it was the second door on the right.

Ryan stepped back through the double doors and headed towards the office, he realised that he could now be walking straight into trouble, especially if he had been spotted on the CCTV jumping the fence. He took out his gun and held it by his side. He saw the office further up and approached it slowly, he listened from the outside when he got close enough to it but couldn't hear anything, he tried the handle, it was locked. He raised his gun and stood to the right of the door and knocked on it, no answer, he lowered his gun again. He thought about kicking the door in but didn't want to draw attention to himself. He carried on up the corridor and came upon another door, it had a window next to it, he crawled beneath it and checked up and down the corridor before raising himself up. The first thing he saw was the back of a head, he ducked back down and waited, the door never opened, he raised up again, it was a man with brown hair, he looked like he was holding something in his hand, he looked beyond him and saw Jane and Michael, tied up sitting against the back wall.

Chapter 46

Ryan was almost positive that Jane had caught a glimpse of him before he ducked down from the window, he stood up quicker this time and nodded to Jane not knowing that the glass was mirrored on the inside. He opened the door and entered confidently, the man who was watching them turned expecting to see Carl, or Peter and was surprised when he saw a man he didn't recognise.

'Who are you?' he said turning the gun from Jane and Michael and pointing it at Ryan.

'Jones sent me up, I have to take the woman to them.' He hoped Jones was still here.

'Jones?' The guy asked.

Shit, Ryan thought to himself. 'Yes, he says I had to hurry.'

He then glanced down at Jane and gave a slight nod.

'No one is going anywhere until I've spoken to Carl,' the man fumbled in his pocket and brought out a mobile phone and started pressing buttons on it.

'That's fine with me, I'm just doing what I'm told.' Ryan paused for a few seconds then continued. 'But I would have made sure those two were tied up first, wouldn't you?' Ryan said looking at Jane.

The guy's face dropped, and his eyes filled with fear at the same time as he turned his head round thinking the worst, he still kept his gun pointed at Ryan. He realised the second he turned his head that it was a trick and spun back around just as quick, but Ryan had moved a foot to the left. The guy adjusted his stance and moved the gun to where the centre of Ryan's chest was now, but it was too late; he didn't see Ryan's fist coming in low from his right and smashing into his side.

Ryan was sure he had broken at least two ribs, the guy

staggered but didn't go down, not until the second hit anyway. Ryan used the momentum of his body and the guy's reaction, he swung his right fist high this time and over the guy's hand that was still holding the gun and hit him on the temple, he fell straight down, his gun dropping from his hand as he did. Ryan lifted it up and stepped over the body, he wasn't dead, but he was definitely knocked out. Ryan leaned down and un-tied Jane, who then un-tied Michael, he handed him one of the guns.

'You ok?' Ryan asked.

'Better now.' Jane replied.

'You still armed?' Ryan asked Jane.

'Yes, they never checked.'

'We have to move soon, they will be back here shortly, I still haven't seen Jones yet, but the place is like a maze.'

Michael finished putting a cable tie on the guy's feet, 'I'm sure there were a few guys outside earlier, we couldn't see anyone because of the glass, but I could hear several voices.'

Ryan looked at the mirrored window and realised why he got no reaction from Jane earlier. They all took out their guns and headed back out into the corridor.

Ryan led the way followed closely by Jane — then Michael at the back, they all walked in unison. When they reached the office door Ryan tried the handle, no harm in trying again, but it was still locked. They carried on past the double doors that led to the reception, they crouched as they passed just in case someone was looking out one of the small windows. Once they reached the corner Ryan took a look round and saw another door halfway along on the left, he turned and told Michael to go and keep a lookout from where they had just come and for Jane to watch his back. He carried on alone, staying close to the wall that the door was on. When he reached the door, he pressed his ear against it, it was cold, he listened closely, he couldn't hear anybody talking, but heard movements inside. He wasn't sure of how many people there could be though, but he had to go in regardless. He turned and waved Jane to come closer and cover him, she did so, holding her gun in both hands and kept close to the same wall. Ryan stepped out into the middle of the corridor and faced the door, he tensed his body and lifted his right leg, he hoped to be able to kick the door off its hinges. He leaned back and was just about to power forward when he heard Michael say his name, he stopped and turned to see that Michael had his free hand in front of his face with his finger at his lips, telling him to be quiet, he motioned them to come over to him, he got up and they made their way back to the double doors and into the reception.

'What's going on?' Ryan asked Michael a little frustrated.

'I heard the meeting room door open and a man shouting, I think it was the guy from earlier.'

Ryan was thinking what to do.

'Ok we stay for a few minutes and see if they pass, if they do, we let them, we have to get inside that room, Jones could be in there.'

They stood for only thirty seconds before they heard someone walking down the corridor. Ryan remembered the receptionist from earlier and spun quickly round to see if she was there, she wasn't, she must have finished for the day. He told the others to stay low as the noise from the corridor got closer. Ryan ducked down low but still could see who was passing, he only saw the side of the man's head for a split second, but he knew it was Peter, the man who had been following him, the man from outside the nightclub.

'It's Peter, we have to follow him, stay close.'

Ryan led them out slowly and stopped them when he reached the corner, he looked round and saw Peter going in through the door he had nearly kicked in — closing it behind him. He told Jane and Michael to follow the same plan as before — he took out his gun and walked down to the door before turning and signalling to Michael. He reached out for the handle, no need to kick it in now, he knew it was open. He heard the voices from inside again, one voice louder than the others, he pushed the handle down and started to open the door when he heard the sound of a gunshot coming from inside.

***

Peter had freed the idiot from the meeting room, he was told by him that a man came in claiming he was sent by Jones, he told Peter that he had never seen him before, Peter knew it must have been Ryan. He handed him a gun and told him to go find Carl and meet him at the hold room. Peter headed into the corridor and back to the hold room himself, he had to get to Jones before Ryan did, no loose ends. He walked past the double doors, he never thought of looking into the reception, he turned at the corner and up to the door, he opened it carefully just in case Ryan had got there first, he hadn't. He closed the door and looked across at Clarke. He was sitting at a small desk in the corner of the room with his feet resting on a chair at the side of it, Jones was sitting at the end of a big rectangular table looking at something on his phone, the man in the hood was sitting opposite him.

Clarke lifted his feet off the chair when Peter looked over at him.

'Is everything under control?' Clarke asked.

'Far from it, Ryan has freed the two of them from the

meeting room and got away, I think they're hiding.'

'Did Sonny get away?'

'I believe he is still being loaded into the container at the moment, we have to make sure they don't get to him.'

'Remember he said, no loose ends, he spoke to you earlier about that, what does he mean?'

Peter never answered, he just nodded slowly, before calmly lifting his right arm. He shot Jones in the side of the head.

Clarke nearly jumped out his seat at the sound of the gun. The man in the hood never moved, he had been expecting it, no loose ends in this job usually only meant one thing. He was just glad it wasn't him, yet. He was reassured when he heard the man say that Ryan had got into the building and freed whoever was locked in the meeting room, he hoped he was close by, as he was sure another bullet would be fired soon, and he would rather not be another loose end.

Chapter 47

Both Ryan and Jane had recoiled at the sound of the gun but both refocused again quickly. Ryan took a step to centre himself and kicked the door hard with the heal of his boot, the hinges buckled as it struggled to stay attached to the frame. He had his gun drawn and at arm's length when he looked in through the door, his momentum from the kick had pushed him back against the corridor wall initially, he had pushed himself off it and took two steps into the room.

Through the smoke from the gunshot, he could make out four men inside, three that were breathing and one lying to his right-hand side, who clearly was not. The first man he saw was sitting at the end of a big table and had a hood covering his head. The second was facing away from him, he could only see the back of his head, but he knew it was Peter, his gun was still drawn and pointed at the head of the man in the hood. Ryan was about to check out the third man who was over in the corner, but he never got the chance. The man in the hood, had very suddenly, stood up, at the same time launching himself forward, lifting the table in the same motion. Whether intended or not, the corner of it clipped Peters arm, this never stopped the gun from firing, but it did change the direction of where it was aiming, which was the hooded man's head. The bullet still hit him, but low on the right-hand side of his stomach.

Ryan never saw the man falling, but before he had even hit the floor, Peter had turned and fired again, this time aiming at Ryan. He saw it coming and ducked, pushing Jane away as he fell back out into the corridor. He shouted for Jane to run as he was scrambling backwards trying to get away, he used his free hand to push himself up from the floor. Jane never got up; she was struggling to get to her feet — she feared for her life. Michael had realised the danger and raced down the hall and grabbed her collar from behind and pulled her up and back, Ryan was too far away to grab.

Peter shouted at Clarke to move, now. He reached the door first and pointed his gun out and to the right and fired before grabbing Clarke who was now at his back, he shoved him out and to the left. The bullet missed Ryan's head by a few centimeters, he was still off balance and couldn't get his gun steady enough to fire back, he knew he was in real trouble as Peter steadied himself to fire at him again when he heard a shot coming from behind him. Peter ducked away and ran up the corridor as Ryan finally got to his feet and to the safety of the corner. He turned again and saw Peter heading through a door further down on the right-hand side, Peter fired a wild shot just as he went through, but it was high and hit the wall. The third man from the room who Ryan hadn't seen was closely following Peter, just as they headed into the room the man glanced back up the corridor. Ryan saw his face, it was him — the man from the café who he had chased to the train and had got away — the smug face that disappeared into the tunnel that he swore he'd see again, and now he had. It didn't look smug anymore though, Ryan thought.

'There is a body in that room, I couldn't identify it but I'm sure they're dead, the man in the hood has been shot too, I think he is still alive but will need medical assistance.' Ryan said to them both out of breath.

'I will head towards the meeting room to block anyone from approaching.' Michael said.

'Ok, be careful.'

Michael headed off, Ryan and Jane went back towards the room, Ryan stayed outside as Jane entered. The room was filled with smoke and there was blood everywhere, mostly from the dead man. She didn't go over to him as she knew he was dead; she checked the man with the hood first. She pulled the hood off and he blinked in the light, she took his hand and checked his pulse, it was weak, she lifted the hood and pressed it against the wound and told him to hold it, he nodded.

Jane then checked the second man; she could see the hole in the side of his head but wanted to identify him. She turned his head a little to see his face. She then shouted for Ryan.

'You need to get in here.'

Ryan came through the door and looked down at Jane, kneeling next to the dead body.

'What is it?' he said.

'Look,' she said pointing at the body on the floor.

Ryan walked over and leaned down closer to see him. It was Jones, he closed his eyes for a second.

'They can't get away,' he said.

'Stay here and call for back up.'

'Wait!' she shouted, but he had already left.

***

Interpol's head office in Lyon was as impressive looking a building as you could imagine, for an intelligence agency. It had moved to Lyon from its original building in Paris in 1989. It employed hundreds of staff in countless departments, from receptionist's, secretaries and desk officers to the countless agents who worked in almost every country all over the world. Oliver had spoken to at least ten of these workers in their headquarters in the twenty minutes he had been on hold, and from at least three different departments before he was put through to a woman called Ellie who introduced herself as an intelligence director. Oliver explained who he was and the reason why he was calling, he then gave Ellie a brief account of the case before explaining that the dead man they found was carrying identification on him that said he was a field agent of Interpol. She asked if Oliver could meet two of her men at the coroners in an hour so they could identify the body and take a statement from him, he agreed and hung up the phone, twenty-five minutes for a three-minute call.

Oliver was now sitting in his car outside the coroner's office. He had not long arrived and was just about to light a cigarette when a car pulled into the space next to him, it had two middle aged men inside. He put his lighter away and got out, they introduced themselves before heading inside. The miserable looking man who had the joy of coming in on a Saturday night to take the body, led the three of them through to the morgue. Klass' body was lying on a table in the middle of the room, it was the only body there. The blood from the hole in his neck had been cleaned up and was now just a black dot.

The two Interpol agents looked through the coroners file and spoke between themselves for a bit. They then discussed with Oliver what had happened, and he told them everything that his team had found out so far. They then confirmed that he was one of theirs, and his name was Klass van de Buuk. Oliver noted everything down to update his own file. Before leaving he told them there was also a mobile phone that had been found at the scene and was believed to be the dead mans but was still with forensics. He told them he would hand it over when they got it back, hopefully in the next few hours.

They all shook hands and thanked the coroner, who didn't acknowledge them before showing them out. The two Interpol agents got in their car and drove away. Oliver took out the cigarette he had wanted earlier and lit it, he leaned against his car and smoked it before getting in and heading home.

Chapter 48

Ryan got to the door that Peter and Clarke had left through and pulled it open, it took him into a storage room, which he entered cautiously. He couldn't hear anything and there wasn't anywhere to hide that he could see, it was full of shelves but had no rooms or hidden corners. On the other side of the room was another door, it was lying open, he thought about going back for Jane and making sure she was ok, but he couldn't waste any more time, he stepped through.

***

Jane had gone back to the man who was still breathing, he was struggling to hold the hood against the wound, Jane helped him with it and reached into her pocket with the other hand and took out her phone to call for back up. She unlocked it but was stopped when head office flashed up, they were calling her, she answered...

'Hi Jane, it's Ellie from head office.'

'Hi.' Jane said slightly confused.

'Can you speak just now?'

'Yes, I was trying to phone my section leader just then when you called.'

'Everything ok?' Ellie replied.

Jane then quickly briefed her boss on the last twelve hours and the situation she was currently in.

'Ok I will send back up from the local office.'

'Thanks.' Jane replied. 'Tell them to hurry.'

'I will, the reason I called you is something I wish I didn't have to do over the phone, but I think you need to know, you have been working with a field agent called Klass.'

'That's correct, yes, is he alright?'

Ellie took a few seconds before speaking again.

'I'm afraid to say that he was found dead late last night, he had been shot in the neck in an alleyway outside a pub.'

Jane's heart sank, she nearly dropped the phone.

'Are you sure?' was all she could say.

'Yes, I'm afraid so, we have identified the body already, I'm so sorry.'

Jane felt a multitude of different things all at once, mostly sadness.

'What pub, where did it happen?'

'It was a small pub in the middle of Düsseldorf.'

'Düsseldorf!' she said loudly, 'I left him in Dortmund yesterday afternoon, do you have any idea what happened?'

'Not as yet but we're working on it now along with the local police, they have sent some of his belongings to us and some to forensics, if anything comes up, we will let you know. We need you to come in for an interview as you were his section leader.'

'Of course, once this is over, send back up quickly please.' Jane said and hung up.

She sat in a daze, how could this be, she couldn't take it in, why was he in Düsseldorf without letting her know and what had he been doing.

She stood up, all of a sudden feeling vulnerable, she had to speak with Ryan. She took a step towards the door when she heard a grunt, she looked down to see the man she had been sitting with gesturing for her to come closer, she hesitated but kneeled back down next to him. He struggled to clear his throat and his voice was weak, but he obviously wanted to tell her something.

Jane leaned in closer.

The man closed his eyes, Jane squeezed his hand and his eyes opened again.

'Tell Ryan that the man he has been hunting, the man who was taken from the café is here in the building, tell him he has to be quick though.'

The man closed his eyes again and he looked like he had fallen asleep. Jane's sadness and confusion had quickly changed to anger, she took the gun from her ankle holder and followed Ryan down the corridor.

Chapter 49

Ryan instantly felt the temperature change as he walked out the storage room door and into what was now the mirror image of the first part of the warehouse that he had gained access through. The main difference, he thought, was that it was almost completely empty, which only made it seem bigger, the vastness of the space and the 100-foot-high ceilings only added to it. As in the other warehouse, the outside wall had the same huge shutter doors, like an aircraft hangar and with the same loading bays leading from them.

Halfway down the warehouse Ryan could see at least four containers sitting side by side, the shutter doors that they were sitting in front of were up. The one in the middle was the only one that wasn't locked over and there was a group of workers working at the back, they were loading it. Ryan could tell that none of them were Peter, even from where he was standing. He couldn't see where else they could be either, apart from a few tyre racks and some scattered moveable carts there wasn't any places to hide. Which made the noise from the gun even more of a shock to Ryan, than it usually would have. It had come from behind him, the noise was escalated dramatically in the open space, it echoed all around.

Ryan dived for cover behind one of the tyre carts and looked back across the warehouse to where the shot had come from. He could see a little smoke in the air near the first loading bay, they must have hidden behind it. Ryan's problem now was there wasn't any way of getting close to them without being a walking target. He looked down at the workers loading the containers, they hadn't stopped what they were doing — never mind run or even react to the sound of the gun.

As Ryan turned back round, he saw the top of

someone's head just peering up above the concrete, he was aware that one of them could be hiding somewhere else but doubted it, Clarke would stay close to Peter.

'We have back up on the way, in a few minutes the place will be surrounded, you should come out now and make this easier,' shouted Ryan.

Before they replied Ryan picked a spot just in front of where he thought they would be and fired into the concrete floor, the bullet bounced off it and carried on into the wall behind the loading bay. He heard it hitting the metal, he also heard Clarke's voice shout out as the bullet just missed them and he knew they were both there.

'In a few minutes you're not going to have a choice, our guys will come in and start firing!' Ryan shouted.

'Ok, ok were coming, just don't shoot.' Peter's voice said from behind the concrete wall.

Peter knew the second they came out into the warehouse that it was a mistake, it was too open for them to get an advantage on Ryan, he had run over to the only place where he could get out of sight and realised quickly after doing so that they were now sitting ducks. The only option he had was to come out and try to make it back to the corridor, but he wasn't quite sure how he would do that.

Ryan was skeptical, he waited with his gun directed at the same point as before and after a few seconds he saw the palm of a hand raise up, then another and he saw Peters head appear and pull himself up onto the warehouse floor. When he got up, he turned and leaned down and hauled Clarke up, they both walked out with their hands in the air.

Why were they giving up this easy? Ryan thought as he approached them slowly, still with his gun on Peters head.

'Keep walking, slowly, I need your guns.'

They both kept walking but never reached for a gun. 'I need you to throw me your guns now!'

Still they walked on, they were heading towards the storage room door, they knew Ryan couldn't shoot them both, not without a few seconds gap in between and they were now twenty feet from the door.

'Stop moving or I will shoot!'

Clarke stopped but Peter kept moving slowly, Ryan fired a shot between the two of them, they both clinched at the noise and Peter stopped moving.

***

Jane was now in the storage room, not exactly sure where Ryan had gone, but she thought she heard shouting as she walked down the corridor. She peered through the door but couldn't see anything, and that's when she heard the shot. She froze before rushing to the door and looked out into the warehouse. She could see Peter and Clarke standing in front of her, they were looking down the warehouse, and weren't holding guns. She stepped through the door with her gun drawn and pointed it at them, still no sign of Ryan yet. Peter heard her but never looked round, she edged her way further into the warehouse, wary with every step, she thought she caught someone out of the corner of her eye on her left, she quickly glanced down to see Ryan, he looked at her with a little relief. She was ready to ask him what he wanted her to do when she spotted another man who was running fast and coming up on Ryan's left-hand side. She didn't notice the gun until he raised it to fire.

'Ryan, watch out!' she screamed and aimed her own gun and fired, her shot was high and wide but was enough to put him off from shooting Ryan in the back.

Ryan dived behind the cage but turned as he did, he settled himself and got the man in his sight and fired, he shot the man in the centre of his chest, his gun fell to the floor. He was one of the workers from the container.

When he knew the man wasn't getting up, he stood up himself and pointed his gun back towards Peter, they were still standing where they had been seconds before Jane fired her gun, but this time Peter had Jane by her hair, with his own gun pointed at her head.

Chapter 50

Michael had managed to reach the meeting room where he had been held earlier, the man who had been keeping watch over them was still in there, waiting, he never heard Michael entering the room. Michael grabbed him from behind and snapped the man's neck, he placed him onto the floor out of view behind the large desk and took his gun. He went back into the hallway and headed further up, it was mostly storage rooms and offices, they were all empty. As he got to the end, he saw a door lying half open, he could hear noises from inside, like a static noise you hear when a television is on, he got close to the door and listened, he could hear someone moving around inside. He peered through the gap between the door and the frame, it looked like the security office, he could see two chairs and a table, on the wall was at least six screens that looked like it had CCTV footage playing on them. As he took a step into the room, he saw the tall man with the blonde hair that had tied him up earlier standing looking at the screens on the wall, he looked closer and saw that he was watching one particular screen very intently, the screen showed a large warehouse, in the middle of it was Ryan, he had his gun pointed at someone or something that was just out of view. Michael saw a man approaching on Ryan's left-hand side but Michael was helpless, he didn't know where the warehouse was or how to get to it. He moved to try and get a better view of the screen but got too close to the door, his foot touched it slightly and the door creaked, the security guy inside didn't hesitate, he grabbed his gun from his belt and turned and fired at the door, Michael got out of the way just in time. He pulled the door shut, trapping him inside, it was the only door to the office. Michael wanted to go and help Ryan but now he couldn't leave, the man would follow him.

'You're trapped, this is the only door out, come out with your hands up but first throw out your gun.'

Silence, nothing happened. 'We have back up on the way, you haven't done anything wrong that we know of so don't make any stupid mistakes.'

After a minute a gun slid out from the crack in the door before a tentative foot appeared, Michael was standing tight against the wall, when he saw enough of the man's head, he smashed his gun into the back of it, knocking him to the floor. Michael dragged him back into the office and tied his hands and feet up, he took the man's keys and locked him inside the office before he left, he looked at the screen on the wall again, Ryan was ok and standing again roughly where he had been with his gun drawn. Michael had to find the warehouse before it was too late.

***

Ryan understood he had to be very cautious, he knew Peter was capable of cold-blooded murder, he had just witnessed it with Jones, minutes ago.

'You don't have to do this, let her go and you can still leave.'

'Your right, I will be leaving but now I'm taking her with me.' Peter replied.

'Backup won't be here for another ten minutes, leave her, you can still get away.'

Ryan knew Jane was in trouble, but he also knew that given a chance she would be clever enough to take it.

Peter started walking for the storage room door, he still had Jane by the hair and was dragging her with him, she was resisting but Peter's size and strength made it hard. Clarke was a few steps behind him, he looked like a rabbit caught in the headlights, he still had the gun in his hand but looked like he didn't know what to do with it.

'If anyone follows me or tries to stop me, I will put a bullet in her skull.'

Peter was now five feet from the storage room door, Ryan had his gun pointed at his forehead but knew if he pulled the trigger Jane would die too, he was running out of time. 'I can't let you leave.' Ryan shouted.

Just as Peter opened his mouth to speak, he was cut off by a loud bang coming from behind him, the next five seconds went by very quickly.

The noise had come from a large red fire exit door on the wall behind them, it was a wooden door that had a bar across it, which meant it could only be used to get from the inside out, when the bar is pressed the bolt inside it releases from the floor and allows it to open. The echo from inside the empty warehouse from the door being opened made it even louder, which is why everyone jumped when they heard it; everyone apart from Ryan that is. Clarke was the first to turn around to see where it had come from, followed by Peter and then Jane. And in that split-second that Peter turned his head, is when Ryan fired his gun, luckily Jane had reacted quicker than the other two and fell to the floor, in turn giving Ryan more of a target to hit.

The bullet hit Peter high in his chest, and before he had even hit the floor, Ryan was already a few feet from Clarke who was still looking behind him. He screamed at him to drop his gun, which he did, and stood motionless. Jane was already up and had taken Peter's gun that was lying next to his body, just in case. She headed over to Ryan who was now standing next to Clarke, he had grabbed him by the neck and took his gun also and was now beginning to tie his hands.

Michael closed the fire exit door over and was now

walking towards them.

'Everything under control I see.'

Ryan almost smiled. 'Talk about good timing,' he said instead.

'You ok Jane?' Ryan said to her as she got close to them.

She never replied, she was focused on Clarke and looked pissed.

'Where is he?' she said angrily.

'Who?' Clarke mumbled.

'I'm not going to ask you again, where is he?'

'I don't know who you mean,' he said again.

Jane took Peter's gun and shot him in the foot, the noise was deafening. Clarke fell to the floor screaming in pain, Ryan and Michael were bemused, Jane leaned down to his side, he was grabbing at his foot.

'Tell me where he is, last chance, I'm not playing around, now tell me?'

Ryan looked up at Michael half looking for any clues, but he was equally confused. Clarke's breathing then changed, short fast breaths. He didn't speak.

She pressed the gun into his neck. 'That's it,' she said calmly.

Clarke tried to slow his breathing as best he could to speak. 'In one of the containers over there.' pointing down the warehouse. As they all turned and looked down, the container that the men had been loading was being closed over, as soon as the lock was sealed, all five of the vehicles started to pull away from the bays and out the huge shutter doors.

'We need to get to the car,' she said grabbing Ryan's arm.

Chapter 51

Michael stayed with Clarke as Jane took off through the storage room door, followed by Ryan, who wasn't quite sure what was going on or who was in the container but clearly Jane knew something he didn't.

They ran down the hallway, past the room where Jones' body was lying, turned left at the corner and out through the double doors into the reception. There was still no one at the desk, they carried on out into the car park and over to the car, which was parked at the far side, the last of the five containers was just leaving through the barrier as they were halfway to the car.

Jane fished the keys out of her jeans pocket as she ran, Ryan got in the passenger seat as Jane started the engine. She put it into first gear and the car burst into life, she crashed through the barrier, cracking the windscreen as she did and took off up to the main road, then took a left and a mile up the road they could see the rear of the last container, Jane floored it.

Ryan didn't want to distract her, so he waited until they were close enough to the container before asking what was going on.

'Who is in the container and why are we chasing them?'

'When you ran after Peter and Clarke I went to see if the man in the hood was still alive, he was weak but alive and wanted to tell me something. I had just got off the phone with my head office in Lyon, Jane took a second to compose herself, they called to say that Klass was found dead last night outside a pub In Düsseldorf…' she turned and looked at Ryan, he put his hand on his head in disbelief.

'I'm so sorry Jane, you ok?' he asked her.

'I will be when I catch the bastard who killed him.'

She continued. 'The man in the hood told me that the man from the café — that we had been sent to watch in the meeting, was in the warehouse, he told me to hurry if we wanted to catch him, that's why I did what I did to Clarke, I had to know where he was and didn't have time to mess about, he can't get away.'

Ryan was thinking about what was going on. He was trying to piece all the bits together but like Jane said they had to stop this container, if they could, and hope that their man was on it.

'Go faster, we need to cut one of them off before they reach the dual carriageway!' She was already doing 130kph.

They were almost on the tail of the last container when its brake lights came on; they were approaching a roundabout. Jane eased of the accelerator slightly as they turned onto it, the roundabout was huge, there was some sort of metal structure in the middle, like a memorial. The container drivers obviously had a plan, the first one took the first exit, the second one took the second exit and so on.

'Shit! What do we do?' Jane shouted.

'Follow the third one.'

The third container took the exit that was heading north, back up through Holland. They followed for almost six miles before Ryan called Michael to see if he could get more information from Clarke, he told him they had tried, and he had sworn he didn't know which container it was, he had then passed out from the pain.

Ryan had no option but to shoot the rear tyre and try to blow it out, he managed to hit it with his second shot. The container pulled into a truck stop and the driver jumped out the cab and lay on the floor with his hands out in front of him. They checked the cab and opened the back doors, but it was just a wall of tyres, the driver had got far enough away now that they couldn't double back and catch any of the other containers. The other four containers would be long gone, even if they arranged a helicopter to be dispatched it would be an hour before it was in the air, and they could be anywhere by then. They placed the driver under arrest and waited for the local police to attend before heading back to the warehouse. The container would be emptied and checked at the station, but they knew the chances were he'd gotten away.

They drove back in silence, both thinking about Klass.

It looked like almost every law enforcement agency in Holland had arrived at the warehouse by the time they returned. The place was lit up with blue flashing lights. They parked the car closer to the main doors and headed into the reception where they were met by Michael.

He explained that almost everyone inside had been gathered up and had started to be questioned, he said that Clarke was on his way to the hospital under armed guard and so was the man in the hood, he said that he hadn't seen him yet but had been informed by an officer. The uniformed officers had done a sweep of the building and came across a very large amount of class A drugs. He also told them that the man who owned the company was a man called Sonny Gilles. He was the man from the café in Amsterdam that had been abducted, Michael had confirmed this with head office. Ryan and Jane looked at each other and lowered their heads.

'That's who was in the container.' Ryan said. 'That's why we took off.'

Michael looked angry, but they weren't sure if it was at not being told or the fact that they didn't catch him.

'There is no trace of any paperwork for those containers anywhere in the building either,' he said.

'The man in the hood, do we know who he is?' Jane

asked.

'No, he had passed out as well but is alive and in critical condition as I said, we will find out soon.'

'We need to question him as soon as possible.' Ryan said.

'I will find out what hospital he is being taken to and when you will be able to speak with him.' Michael replied.

Ryan and Jane made their way into the warehouse, there was people everywhere. They headed for the warehouse the same way they had left, the room where Jones' body lay was filled with people, his body was still where it had been earlier. They passed through the storage room and out into the warehouse, it was also busy with people. The majority of them were standing where Clarke had been shot in the foot by Jane; there was a pool of blood on the floor. Ryan spoke to a forensic officer before heading over to the fire exit door, someone had opened it from the inside and wedged it so they could go back and forth, it took them into the hallway, same white and grey as at the other end. They walked until they reached the first office they came to, there was an officer standing outside it. He told them it was the security office that had the CCTV footage.

'I'm from British intelligence and need to check the tapes to see who or what has been loaded into one of those containers.'

'Yeah, we had the same idea when we got here,' the officer replied. He was a small Dutch man who was wearing a uniform that looked two sizes too small for him, Ryan didn't like his tone.

'What came from this idea then?' He asked him.

'From what we can tell, your counterpart from British intelligence, in his wisdom, locked the security guy inside, when he came around and got his hands free, he deleted all the footage from every camera from yesterday onwards, which really helped.'

Ryan scratched his head in annoyance and walked away without saying anything. They walked past the meeting room that Jane had been held in and back to the reception, the sat on the expensive chairs and sighed at each other with tiredness and frustration.

'Why can't we get a break on this?' Ryan said.

Surely with the number of workers in this place one of them will talk.' Jane replied.

'I wouldn't count on it, if he's been here for a few days, he could have stayed in his office or if he is the man that you said he could be, then there is more chance that everyone would be too scared to open their mouth regarding him or his whereabouts.'

'My head hurts thinking about it, I thought this would have been done with when we got the location of this place from Jones' phone, but it seems to be getting more confusing.'

'Me too, I think we should get some rest and start again in the morning, I will let Michael know to keep in touch.'

Michael told Ryan he would keep him informed if anything changed and to text with the name of the hospital the injured men were headed to when he knew. Michael was going to hang around for another hour or so.

Ryan drove and Jane checked her phone for the nearest hotel, which turned out to be a budget chain hotel five miles away. They drove for ten minutes without speaking before arriving at the hotel, Ryan parked the car. The lady at the reception told them it was only a double room they had available, they both looked at each other half asleep and agreed. They took the elevator up to the third floor; their room was the first one on the left. Ryan opened the door and entered another European hotel room, not so modern or cosy and with no view, but it was clean and warm. Ryan got changed in the room and Jane in the bathroom, they got into bed, Ryan closest to the door, out of habit. Twenty seconds after turning out the bedside light they were both sleeping.

Chapter 52

It was 4 a.m. when Oliver was woken by his phone buzzing. He was tired and annoyed and didn't do the best job of hiding either when he answered. He grunted into the phone.

'Hi Oliver, it's forensics here, we have examined the mobile phone that we collected from the crime scene last night.' A voice said.

Oliver grunted, again, he hadn't got to sleep until 2 a.m. after returning home last night, and as with every new case he had lay awake in bed going over it in his mind.

'We have found blood on it which, not surprisingly came from the victim, as well as some partial fingerprints, again from the victim.'

Oliver really hoped she was leading towards something here.

'After we were finished with it, we passed it to our tech guy — he was just on the phone to say there has been a picture taken with it, pretty recently.'

'Uh huh,' Oliver sat up and reached for his cigarettes.

'They said that it was taken very close to our time of death and that it looks like it could have been taken from the crime scene, you might want to take a look.'

Oliver swung his legs round and sat on the edge of the bed.

'I'm getting ready, I will be there as soon as I can.'

***

He drove slowly, mostly due to the fact that he was still half asleep and the roads were icy, the temperature in the car read minus 5.

The forensic lab was only eight miles away and by the

time he had got there the cold had woken him up a bit.

The forensics officer in charge of the case was waiting for Oliver as he arrived.

'Morning,' she said, a little too happy for the current hour.

Oliver looked at her and smiled.

'Follow me through, one of our tech officers has the image on his computer.' They went into a small office near the back of the building that had a worktop that ran the full length of it, it was divided into five desks by partitions, which separated the computers. There was a middle-aged man in jeans and a lab coat sitting at the last computer in the row, he was sipping from a thermal coffee cup, he shook Oliver's hand and then turned back to his screen.

'This is the image that we got from the phone.'

The picture had been blown up to the full size of the screen but was still small. The picture itself was good for a phone but not for a camera.

'Can you make it any bigger?' asked Oliver, tilting his head to the side, the picture had been captured at a slight angle.

After some tapping on his computer the picture jumped from the computer screen to a large projection screen mounted on the wall in front of them, Oliver took a step back to take it all in.

He knew right away that the picture had been taken by the dead man at the crime scene, it was from the exact place where he had been found. He could see the alleyway and the step leading from the rear of the pub, further up on the right-hand side he could make out the restaurant door where the man who called the police worked. He also knew that this could be a massive piece of evidence regarding the agent's death, and he couldn't quite believe that there was a chance the dead man could have taken it. But that wasn't all, the best part about the image was, that directly in the middle of the picture was the back of a ford pickup truck, and better still, the license plate on it could be seen as clear as day.

In the seventeen years that Oliver had been a detective he couldn't remember ever seeing a picture that appeared like it had been taken by a victim of what could possibly be his killer and possibly the getaway car.

Oliver took the phone and a printout of the image, he asked for a copy to be sent to his email address also, then thanked both of them and headed out to his car and got in. He sat for a few minutes looking at the image and thought of how the last moments of this field agent's life had gone.

He took out his phone and called Interpol head office again, after another twenty minutes he received a call with the number of a Jane Campbell who was the section leader in charge of the agent. He saved the number on his phone but thought better of phoning at this hour, he started the car and made his way home, for the second time tonight.

Chapter 53

Jane woke with the sound of the shower running, she ran her hand through her hair and glanced over at the clock sitting on the bedside table, it was 6:42 a.m. She felt like she had just closed her eyes moments ago. She stretched and sat up in bed, she was about to stand up and grab the house coat that was draped over the chair next to the bed when the shower stopped, she paused.

Ryan spent a few minutes drying off and brushing his teeth before he came out. He had put his trousers on in the bathroom, but his shirt was hanging over the cabinet door in the room.

'Morning, sorry if I woke you.'

'No, it's fine, how was the shower?'

'Refreshing,' he said.

Ryan walked across the room and handed the bathrobe to Jane, she stood up from the bed and took it from him, they looked at each other. They both knew that there was something between them, but deep down they also knew this was not the right time, or situation to do anything about it. They both smiled and Ryan grabbed his shirt, Jane walked to the bathroom and got undressed, she took a long shower and tried her best to clear her mind and concentrate on the day ahead.

She reluctantly got out and changed after fifteen minutes. When she opened the bathroom door, she could smell coffee. Ryan had nipped down to the breakfast room and brought up hot croissants and coffee. She sat on the edge of the bed and took a bite of a croissant and a sip of coffee. Ryan was sitting at the desk drinking his coffee. They both felt refreshed, but both were still thinking about Klass, Ryan wanted to say more to try and make her feel better but felt slightly awkward as he hadn't known Klass for very long.

'Michael called when you were in the shower, he gave me the address of the hospital, he is on his way over himself and says it's not too far from here.'

Jane nodded as she was still chewing the croissant, she took her phone from her jeans pocket.

'Did he say how he was doing?' she asked when she had finished chewing.

'They operated on him not long after he was admitted, Michael says he is doing ok considering, we can see him from 9 o'clock, if he is awake.'

'That's good, I have to make contact with head office first, they want to see me for interviewing because of what happened to Klass. I will find out if it's ok to come in later on today so I can head to the hospital with you.'

Ryan looked at the floor. 'I'm sorry about Klass, I know you worked together for a long time.'

They finished their coffee and got ready to leave. Jane phoned head office and Ryan headed out the back to bring the car round after paying the bill.

Chapter 54

Erasmus University Medical Centre was a twenty-minute drive from the hotel. Ryan was driving the Audi, with the cracked windscreen. The area they were driving through was mostly industrial, it was near a port and the majority of the buildings were either factories or large warehouses. As they drove further in from the outskirts, a town started to take shape, with scattered groups of housing estates, before they eventually reached the town Centre. It was a typical looking main street, filled with busy people and lined on both sides with shops and cafés. The satellite navigation in the car told them to head east, the hospital sat on the edge of the water at the far end of the town, first thing you see or the last, depending on your direction.

Ryan parked the car in the visitor's car park and they both headed for the main entrance. He asked at the reception about who they were there to see and explained who they were before being told what room to head for. The hospital looked like it was full of twenty something's in white lab coats wandering around looking for sick people to help.

'Did you manage to get a hold of head office?' Ryan asked Jane as they waited for the elevator to arrive on the ground floor.

'Yes, they asked me to come in this afternoon and make a statement.'

'Did you say to them about Sonny and what you were told yesterday?'

'No, I left it, until we've spoken to the man this morning, then I can fill them in on all of it.' she replied.

The elevator doors opened — they pressed for the third floor, the doors closed and the motor above their heads hummed and kicked into life and took them up.

Michael was waiting for them when the elevator doors opened again, he looked wired as they approached him.

'I was just about to call you. I got here fifteen minutes ago and was let in to see him not long after, to explain who I was and to take a statement from him but there wasn't any need to.' Michael said.

'What do you mean?' Ryan replied.

'Go see for yourself, he wants to speak to you anyway.'

Ryan looked at Jane and then into the room at the man lying in the hospital bed, he walked in and stood at his bedside, he couldn't quite believe what he was looking at, the man had his eyes shut and a drip attached to his left arm that was supplying him with fluids. He wasn't looking too bad for someone who had took a bullet in the stomach the day before. Ryan stepped closer and reached out and put his hand on his arm, the man's eyes opened when he felt the touch, he looked up at Ryan.

'Hi son.' The man said.

Chapter 55

Ryan took a seat next to his father's bed; he was completely at a loss as to why he was here, how he could be involved in all this and what the hell was going on. Ryan had so many questions to ask him, but his father couldn't stay awake long enough to answer any of them. He spoke to a nurse who had come in to check on him, she said he would be drowsy for another half hour or so.

Ryan shouted on Michael and Jane to come in.

'Is everything ok?' Jane asked.

'Yes, he is still drowsy from the anesthetic but should be awake in a half hour.' Ryan replied.

'Did you manage to speak with him at all?' asked Michael.

'Yes, he said a few words when I first came in.'

'Why did he ask for you?'

'I think more than likely because he is my father.' Said Ryan.

Jane looked at the man in the bed. Michael looked at Ryan.

'He is also your boss.' said Michael.

Ryan turned and looked at his father lying in the bed. 'The one who was taken in Amsterdam?' He asked, looking back at Michael.

'The very one, I think we should find somewhere to talk.'

***

Michael left to ask if there was a room they could use while they waited on Ryan's dad coming around, Jane left to find them all coffee.

They were told they could use a small waiting room next door, Jane brought in coffee from a vending machine, and they all sat waiting for Ryan to speak first.

'Were you aware that our boss was also my father?' He asked Michael.

'No, I had no idea, I'm guessing you weren't aware that he was in charge of the agency?' He replied.

Ryan thought about it. 'No, I knew that he worked for the government, but I didn't know in what capacity, certainly not in intelligence.'

Jane was staring into her coffee, she felt like she shouldn't really be here, she took out her phone and thought about calling her boss and arranging to come in sooner.

'I haven't seen him since I was eleven, I was always told he couldn't be there when I was younger, and he arranged for my grandmother to look after me.'

'I think you have a lot to talk about before we even think about continuing with the case.' Jane said.

'I do but I need to make sure that we don't lose Sonny, for now, that's more important.'

Jane nodded.

They all sat in silence drinking the last drops of their coffee, the room was quiet and small. Inside it had eight chairs in total including the ones they were using; it had no windows and a large television mounted on the wall in the top corner. The television had been on since they came in, but the sound had been muted, Jane stood up and found the remote, she turned the volume up and found an English-speaking news channel. The sport news had just finished and the presenter started going through the local headlines, they were all watching the screen.

The main headline was the upcoming strike that had been planned by the port workers in two weeks' time, the camera cut and went to a man standing next to the water, he was speaking Dutch with English subtitles, he wasn't very happy looking.

The next two headlines were about recent thefts in the area and then the last one was regarding the incident at the warehouse last night, it mentioned the large police presence and the discovery of a very large amount of class A drugs and the following arrests of a number of the warehouse employers, which the police were more than happy with. The screen then cut to footage of the warehouse from last night, it was filmed from in front of the booth at the entrance, you could see the broken barrier that Jane drove through when they chased after the container. They made no mention of the owner or the fact that he had escaped.

They all turned and looked at each other. 'I'm glad that he wasn't mentioned in the report, it still gives us time to track him down, if we can, without everyone following the case.' Michael said.

'But how?' said Jane. 'We're no closer now than we were at the start, he got away.'

The headlines finished and it changed to the weather report, a small man wearing a cream suit, forecast that the recent cold spell had to continue for the next few days with low pressure coming in from the Atlantic that would bring heavy snowfall for most of Europe in the next 48 hours, France and Belgium had to get the worst of it.

Jane turned the volume down just as the nurse came into the room and told Ryan that his father was awake and wanted to speak with him again.

Ryan stood up. 'Let me speak with him for a bit and I will call you both in.'

'Ok,' said Michael.

Ryan's fathers name was John, and he was sitting up in his bed. He looked alert and a lot better than he did earlier, there was colour in his cheeks and he was sipping water from a cup, Ryan sat in the same chair as before.

'Ryan, I have a lot to explain to you.' He paused. 'I

made a choice a long time ago that I have thought about every day since, it was the hardest decision I have ever made, and I hope you can learn to understand this.'

Ryan stared down at the floor, he knew how he felt inside about his father and his upbringing. He wasn't angry towards him but being honest with himself, at that moment, he didn't really feel anything towards him, apart from shock that he was lying here in front of him now.

'I have no complaints about how I grew up and what you did, I am happy that you are alive but most of all I have to catch this man, Sonny. So, you could start with why we have been hunting him down for the last three days.'

As it turned out, both stories were connected. Ryan was seven years old when his mother died, he was told this when he was young but not how it had happened, his father chose not to, but now it was time.

Chapter 56

In 1991, when Ryan's father was in his early twenties, he had been a police officer for three years, he had also just been promoted to a detective and at the time, was one of the youngest to have done so.

He was smart, organised and had natural leadership skills. It wasn't long before he was headhunted by the intelligence services and was moved up to a field agent soon after joining them.

John also had a brother, Alan, who had followed him through the police force and eventually into the agency too. Alan was four years older than John, and although he had much of the same attributes, he wasn't quite the leader that his brother was and for much of the time, lived in his shadow. They had worked alongside each other for a short time, in the field, before John was inevitably moved up the ladder, leaving his brother behind. Alan, in time, started to make a name for himself, all the while holding resentment for his younger brother and after a few years he was eventually promoted to be in charge of his own unit which then became a key asset for the British Intelligence, especially in jobs overseas, on foreign fields. But as time went on his loyalties for his country began to fade and his need for power and money grew. Alans unit had begun to operate beyond their protocol and would freelance their skills for financial gain, the power came later as they became very wealthy.

The majority of the jobs they took were mostly moving either an individual, information or more often than not large amounts of cash across borders and into countries that important people didn't have access too. They did this mostly in Europe where they spent most of their time working for the agency, but as time went on people started to notice certain things that weren't adding up.

The problem that John had, who was now intelligence director by this point, was that the unit his brother was in charge of were like brothers, he couldn't get to any of them to talk on their own and they were as smart as any other of the agents in the agency. Eventually John had to set up a secret unit that tracked all their movements, he knew it would end the relationship he had with his brother but at this point there wasn't much of it left anyway. It took six months of tracking before John had a case to take to his seniors who in turn issued a warrant for Alan's arrest.

Two days before the secret unit were to make a raid on Alan and his team, Alan got wind of it and went into hiding, John never found out how he knew they were coming but he guessed they must have been tipped off by someone within the agency. The unit was de-classed, and warrants released for everyone involved in Alan's team, the issue was now trying to locate them, they were scattered all across Europe by then.

Twenty-four hours later was when everything changed for good.

Chapter 57

Ryan couldn't remember his uncle, but he knew he must be involved in some way for his father to be telling him now.

John received a call from his wife, Katie, a few days after his brother had gone into hiding, saying that his brother Alan had appeared at the door of their home. She had taken Ryan to his grandmothers for the night and got back home just as he knocked on the door, she told John that Alan had been drinking by the looks of things, she had called John when he went to the bathroom and spoke quietly, so Alan couldn't hear her.

John told her he was on his way, but it would be just over an hour before he got there, he told her to try and get him to leave and that he would send a local police car to the house, who would hopefully be there sooner than him.

Katie came off the phone and turned to see Alan standing next to the dining room table, he had taken out a bottle of red wine from the wine rack and sat two glasses on the table. He poured two drinks and asked her to join him, she sat down but told him she wasn't feeling very well and didn't want to drink.

At first, he was friendly and spoke the way he did when she had first met him and they used to socialise together, but that changed with every drink he took. By the time he had drank his third glass, anger began to creep out, he would be overly affectionate one minute then explode into bursts of rage the next. She took the glass he had poured her and drank it, she asked for another just to stop him from drinking so much but left it sitting in front of her, when the bottle was finished though he just fetched another one and poured another glass. He began saying things about himself and John that she never understood, things about work and the way their lives had turned out, he was beginning to drift in and out of sentences, slurring his words, she hoped that John would be here soon or that Alan would pass out and she could run to her mother's house.

She checked the clock on the wall in the kitchen, it had been 35 minutes since she phoned John, he still wouldn't be close. She started to panic a little as Alan's anger only grew. She stood up from the table and he asked where she was going, she told him to the bathroom as she walked past him, he grabbed her arm as she passed, she looked at the clock as he was about to say something, but he stood up and pulled her closer to him, he was hurting her arm. He asked why she was constantly looking at the clock, he knew John was at the office that day and was sure he wouldn't know he was here. I came here to fix things with John he said, he picked up his wine glass with his free hand and drank the contents before dropping the glass on the floor, but he had since changed his mind and knew it could never be sorted, deep down, John had stabbed him in the back, his own brother, that's how he saw it anyway.

He wanted Katie to tell John he would be going away for a while and he wouldn't see him again, she saw a glimmer of hope that he wanted her to pass on a message. She tried to wriggle free from his grip but he grabbed her by the throat, she slapped him in the face which he didn't react very well to, he punched her in the mouth and split her lip, she fell to the floor crying.

***

It was a wild night and John was driving as fast as he could, he didn't think for a minute that his brother would hurt his wife, but he knew that him turning up at his house was not good and he didn't want Katie to be in that situation. He was driving as fast as the conditions would let him, he nearly slid of the road a few times, but he had to get home to his wife.

***

Katie became terrified after he had actually hit her, she never thought he would have ever done that to her. She then made the mistake, out of fear and panic, of telling him that when he was in the bathroom earlier that she had phoned John at his office and told him that he was here, she told Alan that he had left straight away and would be here any minute. Alan turned and looked at the clock on the kitchen wall, his eyes were blurry from the wine but he knew it was about forty minutes ago that he went to the bathroom, it was too early, he turned back around to face Katie, just as she swung her arm with all her strength and hit him on the side of the head with the empty wine bottle from the table, she'd managed to grab it when he'd turned away. He stumbled backwards and fell onto one knee, Katie took off for the front door, she pulled it open and ran out into the rain, the wind nearly pushed her off her feet. She ran down the path and tried her car door that was in the driveway, it was locked. She carried on to the end of the path and turned towards her mother's house, she screamed, but the noise from the wind and the rain easily drowned it out. She took off, heading up the hill but was too late. Alan had got back to his feet and caught up with her, just as she had begun to run, he punched the back of her head and she hit the ground face first.

Katie woke up after ten minutes, she felt sick and dizzy. She was sitting in the passenger seat of what she thought must be Alan's car, they were speeding through country roads that led away from her house. She had blood on her face, she could feel it, she thought about jumping out of the car, but the speed Alan was driving at she knew she would have been killed instantly.

She pleaded with him to slow down, she begged him, but he was filled with alcohol and rage and wouldn't listen, she told him it wasn't too late, but he looked straight ahead like he never heard her. Katie looked out at the darkness in front of her, it was lit up in little bursts of light from the cars headlights as it twisted and turned. She looked back at Alan as he took a sharp corner too fast and the car skid, the next corner came too quick after that and the car skid again but this time it hit a small fence at the side of the road and flipped into the air. It landed on a grass verge on the other side of the fence and rolled down an embankment. It came to a stop on its roof in a small river at the bottom.

Chapter 58

Ryan had listened to his father speak about his mother without knowing who she really was. Sometimes he thought he could remember her but knew he might be confusing the memories with pictures or home videos he had seen of her. Regardless of this, he had felt emotional when his father mentioned her, and he felt a different kind of anger when he knew how she had died. He could tell his father was emotional too but neither of them showed it.

Ryan stood up and filled his father's cup with water and sat back down.

'So, then what happened?' Ryan asked.

John explained how he had arrived at the scene fifteen minutes later, he saw the police car parked by the side of the road and stopped, a passing car had seen Alan's car flip over the fence and down the embankment.

John told the policeman who he was and jumped over the fence and scrambled down the embankment and into the river. Katie was lying half in and half out of the passenger side of the car, he knew immediately that she was dead. He kneeled in the water next to her and lifted her head and wiped the hair from her face, he let out a scream, he lay her back down and ran to the driver's side, he pulled the door opened but his brother wasn't there. He walked back around the car and headed up the embankment and shouted at the police officer where the other body was, the officer told him it was only the woman that had been found at the scene. He slumped to his knees and began to cry, after a few minutes he began ordering a search of the area, the driver had to be found now.

Over the next day a full police search was carried out, aided by British intelligence. They checked the local area, knocking on all doors within a five-mile radius and they also put his picture out to all airports, train stations and hospitals. John knew though that with Alan's contacts from his job that he had many options and friends that could help get him out the country, without them knowing, but he had to try. After seventy-two hours the search was stopped, and John knew for sure he had gotten away.

For the next few years John tried his best to raise Ryan and run the agency, it was hard and through time John realised that it wasn't fair on Ryan, he wasn't getting the proper childhood that he deserved and being honest with himself, he was never that close with his son, because of his job, it was his mother who had raised him and allowed John to concentrate on his career.

So, with a lot of regret, he decided that the best thing for his son was to give Katie's mother full custody of the boy, she was the one who had watched him for most of the time since the death of his wife. He knew it was for the best, but it didn't make it any easier to do.

'I want you to know that I never gave up on you Ryan, I just couldn't give you what you needed.'

Ryan sat with his head down. 'I don't blame you for what you done; it is what it is.'

'I'm sorry regardless.' said his father.

Chapter 59

Oliver's alarm sounded at its normal time — he hit snooze for an hour before getting up. He showered, got dressed and was sitting at his breakfast bar in his kitchen eating a slice of toast with a strong coffee. He took out the image from last night of the alleyway and stared at it, he was still amazed that the picture had been taken at the time of the dead man's last moments. He lifted his mobile and walked out onto his balcony and dialed the number for Jane Campbell, the team leader of Interpol. It was just after ten o'clock in the morning.

'Hi, who is speaking?' Jane answered, herself and Michael were still in the waiting room.

'Hi, my name is Oliver Stam, I am the lead detective in charge of the case involving the death of one of your agents, is this Jane?'

'Yes, it is, how can I help you?'

'I received a call early this morning from our forensics team, they had taken some possessions from the crime scene for analysis, one of the items that was tested was a mobile phone that we believe belonged to the agent. After it was tested and confirmed that it was only the deceased's DNA that was on the phone it was passed to their tech officer. Once he had examined it, he came across an image that had been taken. They phoned me in the middle of the night to go over and have a look and I'm almost positive that the image has been taken from the crime scene, and I believe that it was taken close to the time of the man's death. It shows the alleyway outside the pub where his body was found but more importantly, it shows the rear of a car that looks like it's driving away from the scene.'

Jane stood up and headed out of the waiting room.

'What kind of car is it?' She asked.

'It's hard to tell but I would say some kind of 4x4.'

'Can you send me the photo please.'

'Sure, give me your email and I will send it over straight away.'

'Thank you for this, if we can get any information from it, I will let you know.' Jane said.

Oliver got off the phone and sent the image before picking up his jacket and heading into the office.

Jane received the email and looked at the image on her phone, but it wasn't big or clear enough. She then asked the hospital reception if it was possible to forward the image onto them and if they could print it off, which they did. When she had the image, she went to find Michael, she showed him the picture that had been taken and explained the phone call she received from Oliver.

'Does this place mean anything to you?' Michael asked her, looking at the picture closely.

'No, but the car in it looks familiar, although I don't recognise the license plate.'

The both of them looked at the picture again, studying the car.

'We need to show Ryan this, we need to interrupt them.'

***

John was starting to get tired but wanted to tell his side of the story and tell Ryan what he knew to help with the case.

'So, what came of your brother, Alan?' Ryan asked.

John took a sip of water and cleared his throat.

'That was also part of the reason I decided to give custody to your grandmother. Although I had dealt with the grief and regret of your mother's death, I still couldn't live with the fact that the person who killed her was out there somewhere, living his life. I wanted to find him but the last thing I wanted was for anything to happen to you.'

'And did you ever find him?' Ryan asked.

They were interrupted as Jane knocked on the door and opened it a little, she put her head in and apologised and asked if she could speak with Ryan.

'Yes, come in, I was just about to call on you both.'

Jane and Michael came in and grabbed a chair and sat next to Ryan.

Ryan introduced Jane to his father before asking her what she needed to talk to him about.

'I got a phone call from the detective in charge of Klass' murder, he sent me this picture that was taken on Klass' mobile, and from what the detective says, it was where his body was found.'

She passed it to Ryan who stared at it.

'How could this be?' said Ryan.

'The detective thinks that after Klass had been shot in the neck he managed to crawl onto his front and somehow take this picture.'

Ryan didn't take his eyes off it; he was trying to imagine how Klass could have been able to take this picture in his dying moments — if that was what he had actually done.

'Is this the same car from the club?' he asked Jane.

'I thought it was too, but I don't think it's the same license plate.'

'It's not, these plates are Dutch but the ones we checked from the car leaving the club were German,' he paused, 'it does look like the same car though, I agree.'

'Did we ever get any number plate recognition hits on the German plate from earlier?'

'Yes, but it was only from Germany, mostly around

the Dortmund area.'

'Ok, call this one in too and hopefully we get a hit on this as well, which will hopefully help us find out who it belongs to and where it has been recently.'

Jane called it in before sitting back down.

John asked to see the photo and was sitting in bed staring at it.

'I'm sorry about your agent Jane, thinking about it now, I might have been there when it happened, and I think I know who killed him.'

Chapter 60

'How's that?' Jane asked him.

'After I was abducted from the side of the canal in Amsterdam, I spent twenty-four hours in the back of a van, it only stopped once for fuel before stopping at what I managed to work out, was a pub in Germany. Whenever the door to the room where I was held was left open, I could hear German being spoken and the overwhelming smell of beer. I had been there for two days when the men who had taken me there left and two new guys took over, one of them was Dutch and the other English. They were with me for around twelve hours before I was moved again, this time I was led out the pub and into what I thought was a 4x4.'

Michael, Jane, and Ryan were all listening intently.

'As I was put into the back of the car I could hear voices outside, there was a commotion, I had the hood over my head at all times so never saw anything, but what I thought I heard moments before the two of them got into the car alongside me was the sound of a gunshot, then one of them mentioned something about a breadcrumb.'

Ryan thought about the picture, and the car, and what his father had said.

'Could it have been Peter and Jones?' Ryan said.

'Quite possibly.' replied John.

'This car has to be involved in all this, if it is the same car then we know that it left the pub in Düsseldorf and ended up at the warehouse in Rotterdam, we know that because that's where John ended up.'

'And if it was, there is a chance that the vehicle is still there or being held by the local police as evidence,' replied Michael.

Michael got up and phoned his contact who was still at

the warehouse, he came back after a few minutes.

'The car is still at the warehouse, it's a dark blue ford pickup, it was getting ready to be loaded onto a transporter and took to the local station to be checked for evidence. My contact has stopped it and checked the plates, it's the same as the ones in the picture.'

Ryan was right.

'He said there was also a spare set of license plates in the boot compartment, they were German, ERH V605'

'Now we're getting somewhere.' Ryan said.

'All we need now is a phone call to say if they got a hit on the Dutch plate.' Jane said. 'I will give them another ten minutes.'

Ryan looked at the photo again and thought about how much Klass has helped them by taking it.

Chapter 61

Ryan decided not to mention what he and his father had been talking about before Jane and Michael came in, but he did want them to hear the information on the case and on Sonny, which is why he was going to call them both in before Jane interrupted them.

John began to describe how he came across Sonny.

'Just over three years ago I was at a meeting in Eindhoven with members of the Dutch Intelligence service, we were discussing ways we could work together to break down the illegal drugs that were being imported into Britain. We spoke about different methods of how to stop them at customs and how we could be more stringent in our tactics towards tracking the ways they were being smuggled in. I was then shown two files regarding two of the biggest dealers in Holland. The first was a man who used to run the drugs trade in almost all of Holland but a few years ago he lost his hold on a lot of his men to another gang which had moved in and had begun taking over.

The man in the second file I was shown was the head of the new gang. The only picture they had of him was an old image of who they knew as Sonny Gilles, they said he was in Holland illegally. Over the last ten years he had gone from being a small-time dealer, to running illegal drugs across most of the city Centre.

From there he gradually got the right men on his side, and with a combination of being very clever and ruthless in the same measure, he eventually worked his way through the ranks and became the biggest and most feared drug dealer in Holland and anyone who didn't work with him, or went against him, would end up dead.

After working this way for many years, he made sure he had men around him that he could trust and run his operation for him and so he fell back into the shadows and concentrated on cleaning his money and becoming legitimate. He bought the tyre wholesaler in Rotterdam a few years ago knowing it would bring more attention to him but, he had to take the risk.'

John stopped and took another drink.

'They estimated that he had murdered or at least organised the murders of almost a hundred men to get to where he was, but what they didn't have was any information regarding his past or background, where he came from or who he was, but I knew.

His real name was Alan Snow, he was my brother.'

Ryan never said anything, he gripped the chair that his hand was resting on, he could feel his heart beating in his chest, he clenched his jaw. He had been so close to catching him, now he had to find him, he would stop at nothing.

Jane and Michael looked at each other in shock.

'What can we do now?' Michael asked to break the silence.

'Since I found out his whereabouts, I have been monitoring him, for personal reasons more than anything. I knew that Dutch intelligence were closing in on him and that Interpol were aware of him also. So, I tried to stay hidden and make sure he didn't disappear again. The trouble we all had was how rarely he was seen out in public. So, when we got the tip-off of the meeting at the café, I had half an idea that it could be a setup, which as we all know now it was. Even so, we couldn't let the chance go by to possibly catch him, that's why I was in Amsterdam myself. As it turned out this was what he wanted though, he knew if I was aware of who he was, which I'm sure he found out through Jones, that I would be there.

He also made sure that Ryan was the one who got

assigned the case and would be at the meeting place too. Although I tried what I could to stop Ryan reaching the city,' he looked at Ryan, 'the woman at the airport was my doing, but it seems your as stubborn as your father.' Ryan never looked up.

'We assume now that he had planned on making it look like he had been abducted from the café in Amsterdam, which might have been set up as a genuine abduction as I found out earlier today that a car was found burnt out six miles outside of Amsterdam that had four bodies inside. The car was caught on recently installed CCTV in a golf course car park being swapped over from the same car that sped away from the café with Alan inside, so that makes me think he wanted it to appear real and for everyone to think he was dead, but he then had to kill any witnesses and destroy the evidence. The real reason for the elaborate plan, I believe was to bring me out into public where they could abduct me and begin to lay a trap for Ryan to track me down and eventually end up at the warehouse where he could kill both of us.'

'But why?' said Jane. 'Couldn't he have just left and gone into hiding into some other country?'

'I have thought about that and the only thing I can think of is his family back in Britain, he has two grown up kids and a young grandchild. He must be planning on smuggling himself back there to be with them but knows he would always be looking over his shoulder if he didn't kill us.'

'Do you think he will still go ahead with the plan if you aren't dead?' Jane asked.

'He has to, and right now he doesn't know if either of you are alive or dead. If that is his plan then he has no other options, but there are lots of ports he can cross into Britain, how can we tell which one he will use.' Michael said.

They all sat in silence thinking about everything they had been told. The last four days had seen them running in circles chasing who had turned out to be Ryan's uncle, they had been led along from the start, Jane could see the anger and hatred in Ryan's eyes.

'So, what now?' said Jane.

After a long pause Ryan spoke.

'We know that he left the warehouse in the back of a container, he had five of them loaded and leave at the same time as a decoy, we followed one of them, but he wasn't in it. We have to go on the belief that he is heading for Britain, but we can't let that happen.'

Jane's phone started ringing, which interrupted Ryan, she answered it and stood up and listened for a minute.

'We got a hit on the plate Klass got on camera, it's registered to a small accounting firm in Brussels, which isn't a surprise. It was spotted on an automatic number plate recognition system yesterday on several cameras on the main road from the German border to Rotterdam, and again through Belgium and into France two days ago, the strange thing is that it had no hits in Germany, like it disappeared when it got to the border.'

'They changed the plate when they were going into Germany.' Ryan said. 'Incase it was spotted and checked around the Dortmund area.'

'It was spotted in Calais twice in an hour, that was three days ago, once heading towards Calais and the second time heading away from it, the second time they said there was two people in the car and only one on the way down. They checked the CCTV and zoomed in on the car.'

'He must have been going to pick someone up?' said Michael.

'Jones?' Ryan said. 'It must have been Peter; he drove

to Calais to pick up Jones when he arrived and drove him back to Dortmund.'

'I wish it was me who had killed that bastard in the warehouse yesterday,' said Jane.

'I don't understand why he would have drove all that way just to pick up Jones, why not let him get the train to Germany, he must have been going for some other reason too,' said Michael.

'Maybe, it is a long way to go to pick someone up. Phone your guy again and ask him to check all CCTV around the customs depot and the Eurostar drop off, we need to know if it is Jones he has picked up and if he stopped anywhere else.' Ryan said.

Jane phoned them back for an update. She got off the phone and said, 'the car was seen leaving the Eurostar café, two men got in and the car drove away, they have confirmed that Jones was the passenger. They said the time between the second and third camera on the approach to Calais takes eight minutes to drive between, at the average speed limit, it took him eight minutes twelve seconds on the way towards Calais but it took sixteen minutes forty-nine seconds on the way back.'

'They must have stopped somewhere?' said Ryan. 'Michael, can you get hold of Jones' mobile phone or laptop and check its movements for the last four days — if he had them turned on, we might be able to pinpoint a location where they stopped and hopefully why.'

Chapter 62

Sonny was freezing, he was as cold as he had ever been in his life but at the same time relieved. He knew that he had gotten away ok and was through customs, the money he had paid the officer at customs had been worth it. He was on the water and had been for a few hours so he knew he would be back in Britain before long but also that there was less chance of being stopped in Calais than there was in Dover, but even then, his man said they would make sure of an easy passage there as well. He closed his eyes and tried to sleep, another fifteen hours and he would be home again.

***

Jones body was lying in a morgue at a hospital on the other side of the water from the one John was in, Michael had been put through to the forensics officer who was in charge of his body and who had his belongings, she told him she would take his phone to their tech guy and run a trace on it right away and phone back as soon as it had been done. Michael told her he was running against the clock and would appreciate that.

***

Ryan had decided that he and Jane should make their way to Calais, it could be a coincidence that Peter had been to the biggest channel crossing port a few days ago, but Ryan doubted it. If Sonny was making his way into Britain, then this could very well be where he planned to enter from.

'I hope you get better soon; I will be in touch but we need to head to Calais, this has to be connected to Sonny somehow and we are running out of time.' Ryan said to his father while Michael was on the phone.

'I agree, if I hear anything, I will let you know. And I must tell you of the importance of catching this man, there has been a lot of authorities trying to get hold of him for a very long time, including myself. He must not get away, he must be brought in and made accountable for his crimes.'

Ryan nodded.

'Good luck.' John replied.

'Can you phone Jane as soon as you hear back from your contact?' Ryan said to Michael.

'Sure,' replied Michael.

Ryan and Jane left the hospital and got into the Audi, Ryan drove, and Jane checked her phone for the quickest route to Calais. She typed it into the cars satellite navigation, it said traffic was light and they would get there in three hours, Ryan said he could do it in two and a half.

***

After Michael came off the phone with the forensics officer who was examining Jones' body, he asked at the reception what ward the second man who had been brought in last night was in, he told the woman his name was Clarke, she told him what floor he was on, and he went looking.

As it turned out he had been operated on for longer than John — when Jane shot him in the foot she had managed to shoot just behind his two biggest toes, and on the thinnest part of the foot, this had meant that the bullet had gone straight through into the bone and out the other side and just for good measure, had nearly blew both the toes off in doing so. He needed reconstructive surgery to build his foot again. He was still heavily medicated when Michael finally found his room, the local police officer recognised Michael and told him what he knew, there was a detective sitting waiting on him coming around from the anesthetic. What he reported so far, was the man was not cooperating and wouldn't speak to anyone regarding the incident at the warehouse, two more officers tried and failed also. Michael knew he wouldn't fare any better and returned to speak to his boss about their next move, he just got out of the elevator when his mobile started ringing, it was the forensics officer in charge of Jones' body.

'Hi, Michael speaking.'

'Hi it's forensics again.'

'Hi, thanks for rushing this through.'

'No probs, we would have been quicker with it, but the dead man had two mobile phones on him. The first one we checked had all tracking and mobile data turned off, like it was in airplane mode, but with the second phone we managed to get a hit. It looks like he had been busy, we have the phone popping up in France, Germany, Holland, and Belgium. We broke it all down and found that in Belgium he never stopped, he was just travelling through, Germany was mostly spent in Dortmund with a twelve hour stop off in Düsseldorf.'

Klass was killed outside the pub in Düsseldorf which could explain this, and John also said he was held for twelve hours somewhere in Germany, which meant Jones had been there when Klass was killed right enough.

'From Düsseldorf to Rotterdam he never stopped in between, the only other thing that really stands out is when he was picked up in Calais, he travelled for five minutes before cutting off the main road and sat at what we think is a small industrial estate just off the motorway.'

'That could be something, is it possible to send me the location along with the exact time and date of when he stopped?' Michael asked a little more hopeful.

'Sure, I will send it right away.'

Michael ended the call and sat in the small waiting room, impatiently hanging around for new information coming through.

Chapter 63

Ryan and Jane had been driving for just over an hour and were making good time, they had already passed into Belgium and were almost in France.

'How are you feeling about Sonny being your uncle?' Jane asked, they hadn't spoke about it until now and Jane thought she had to ask.

'I'm not sure yet, he planned to kill me and very nearly killed my father too, so regardless of what my relationship with him is, I have to catch him — and I can't stop until I have.'

He didn't want to mention his mother to Jane just yet.

'We will get him, for Klass as well,' she said.

Jane's phone rang, it was Michael.

'Hi Jane, I'm just off the phone with my guy, he is sending me a location, time, and date. He says it looks like they made an unusual stop on the way back from Calais, it was for just over five minutes.'

'Maybe picking up food?'

'We doubt it, it was close to the entrance of an industrial estate just off the motorway, we also saw them leaving the Eurostar café not long before that.'

'Ok, great,' Jane replied.

'I will forward the details onto you when I have them.'

'Thanks Michael, I will check it out before we arrive, we will be in touch.'

'Speak soon.' Michael said and hung up.

Over the next twenty minutes Jane had managed to get an aerial plan on her phone of what was, in fact, an industrial estate ten minutes outside of Calais and just off the main road between the border control. She had also managed to get the names of all the businesses that had units in the estate and pinpointed three buildings that if Jones' phone location was accurate, would look onto it.

It took a further forty-five minutes driving at 120kph before Ryan signaled and turned off the motorway, there was a winding road about half a mile long that led up to the industrial estate. The estate looked like it had been recently built, the large steel buildings looked clean and the grounds maintained, so they hoped it would have CCTV.

It took them a few moments to figure out where Jones would have been located but when they did, it meant they could rule out one of three buildings Jane had found. It was pointing in the opposite direction from the location. The first place that they tried which would have been at the best angle was a furniture store. They went in and checked, but the only camera they had was internal and was positioned to capture the front door but because of its angle, no further.

They walked across to the second place which was a bathroom fitting company, they were shown through the back by a fed-up looking middle-aged man who they presumed to be the owner. He clicked on his monitor and rewound the tapes to the date and time that Jane gave him. It turned out he had two cameras at the front of the building, one was looking down at the main entrance, the second covered the supplies door that pointed out from the side of the building, it was from this one that they got a result.

After skipping through the tape to the rough time, they saw a dark-coloured jeep coming into shot, it had two passengers inside but was too far away to identify who they were.

The jeep parked in a space and after a few minutes the driver stepped out and walked around to the front of the car, he sat on the bonnet — Ryan knew that it was Peter. A few seconds later another man then appeared from the right of the screen and approached him, he was a similar height to Peter, maybe a little taller and had dark hair, he must have already parked his car before Peter arrived. They spoke for a few minutes before Peter passed him some type of bag, they then shook hands and Peter headed back to the car. The other man walked out of shot again but thirty seconds later a car passed by where they had been stood and turned to exit the estate. It was hard to make out, but Ryan thought it looked like an old Peugeot or Renault. Jane took a picture of the clearest image they could get on her phone to send in to head office, hopefully they would be able to enlarge and clean it up and get a license plate number from it. They ran the tape on another thirty-five minutes at a faster speed before another car left, so they assumed the old car that passed first belonged to the man Peter had met with.

Chapter 64

Sonny knew the ferry had docked, the swaying and banging had stopped and the sick feeling he'd had since it set sail started to ease. The time he had spent inside the steel box was hell, but it had given him a chance to think about things, mostly back to when all this had started with his brother. Over time he was aware that he hadn't been as smart and as honest as his younger brother, but he also believed in life taking people down their own path, and his had been to Amsterdam and that is what he had done. He knew he had done things other people wouldn't dream of, but the way he saw it was that he had to survive. He didn't have any regrets about how his life turned out, but he did have one regret — on that rainy night back in England, when he had got into his car with his sister-in-law and drove. He didn't know what he was going to do or where he was going but he didn't plan or ever intend, for Katie to end up dead. He closed his eyes and shook the thought away. All he wanted now was to get back home with his own family and make up for lost time.

***

Ryan and Jane left the industrial estate and carried on to the border crossing, Jane had sent the image away and they knew they wouldn't hear anything for at least thirty minutes. Ryan parked the car outside the Eurostar café, and they headed inside. They sat at a window seat close to the one Jones and Peter had sat days earlier, they both ordered coffee and a baguette and waited.

'What are the chances of us finding out who this guy is? That picture of the license plate wasn't great,' asked Ryan.

'I have sent a lot worse images in than that and still got a result; we just need to be patient,' she replied.

'What are you going to do when this is all over — if it's ever over?'

Jane looked out at the sea.

'I've known since we left the station building in Dortmund that if we ever caught this man, that British intelligence were going to be the one to bring him in, I have only really been tagging along to help you out.'

Ryan smiled at her.

'After everything your father told us earlier, it made it even clearer.'

'How will your boss be if that is the case?' Ryan asked.

'I will have some explaining to do, but in the end, if he is off the streets then it's a win all round, plus we picked up Mr. King back at the café in Amsterdam,' she paused. 'Then I'm due a holiday which I plan on taking, I fancy Majorca maybe.'

'I've heard it's nice,' said Ryan.

They finished their coffee just as Jane's phone lit up, it was sitting on the table next to her mug.

'We got him, let's go.'

They had already paid their bill in case they had to leave in a hurry, Ryan drove again, Jane got in the car and started typing into her phone.

'His name is Graeme Mooney; his car was registered to an address in Wimereux, just south of Calais. He was born in London and served in the British army, he moved to France eight years ago and started working with customs not long after that, he is a shift manager there.'

Jane saved the image of Graeme onto her phone while Ryan tried to navigate his way through the one-way roads and no entries in the border control grounds, it was like a maze. He found a space near the visitors building and headed up the stairs, Jane pressed a bell on top of the counter which made a high-pitched ring, after a few minutes waiting a young woman bounced around the corner.

'Hi, how can I help you?' she asked in English.

'We are here to speak with an employee who works here, his name is Graeme Mooney, can you find out if he is working just now?' Ryan said.

'Hang on, I have to check with my supervisor to be sure,' she said, and left.

'Do we tell them who we are — if they ask?' Jane said to Ryan when she left.

'Not if we don't have to, if this guy gets spooked and runs, we are back to square one, again. Let's see what they say first.'

The woman came back again a minute later.

'Can I ask what this is regarding please?'

'No.' Ryan replied.

She wasn't quite sure how to continue.

'It's a private matter that is in everyone's best interest if only those involved be included in, Mr. Mooney is one of those people.'

'Ok, he is due his break in five minutes, I have told him you are here, he says he will get you out front.'

'Thanks for your help.' Jane said.

Chapter 65

Ryan headed back down the steps, followed by Jane. They leaned against a walled garden outside the front of the office. Ryan was restless again, there was too many delays and hold ups and he needed to get answers soon, he was running out of time.

'You think he will see us?' Jane asked.

'He better, if he isn't out here in five minutes I'm going in there and dragging him out.'

Jane was about to say something when a car pulled up to the barrier just up the road from the offices where they were sitting. She couldn't identify the driver, but she could tell it was a man. The barrier lifted and the car pulled away.

'Does that car look similar to the one in the footage, from the industrial estate we saw earlier?'

Ryan looked up and saw a beat-up old Renault Clio turning out of the office car park and onto the main road.

'It does,' he said as he pushed himself off the wall and began running for the Audi, Jane following close behind.

Ryan started the car and pulled out onto the road, nearly hitting a passing car as he did, the man driving it blasted his horn. The Clio might have been old, but it could still shift, it must have been a sports model back in the day.

Ryan weaved in an out of the traffic, trying to catch him up. The Clio didn't head for the motorway though, he headed west, on a coastal road which was single lane, this meant Ryan had to be patient.

It took him nearly four miles but eventually he overtook a truck and came up behind the Clio. Ryan gestured to the driver to pull over, but this only made him speed up, he was now driving too fast for the road. They had just passed through a small town and were now driving in the countryside, Ryan could see further up the road now, it was mainly fields and what looked like a farm up ahead. He could see that the landscape flattened near the entrance to the farm so he got as close to the Clio as he could as they approached its entrance, he needed to stop him but he needed him alive, so he decided on nudging the back right corner of his car as it braked to take the bend, the slight touch sent the car into a spin, the driver fought to keep it on the road but it was no use. The car spun 360 degrees and skidded into the driveway of the farm and carried on into the field next to it.

Ryan stopped the car in the driveway and jumped out, the driver was shaken, but as his car stopped spinning, he got out and took off towards the farm. Ryan had a head start on him though, and he only got twenty feet before Ryan caught up to him, he tackled him around the waist and took him to the ground.

Jane handcuffed him and dragged him back to the Clio that was lying in the field, he was kicking and screaming, trying his best to get himself free.

Ryan punched him in the mouth, mainly to shut him up.

'I was going to be civilised with you about this, but you blew that by running on us.'

He was still shocked and full of adrenalin from the car spinning of the road.

'I did everything you asked, the container got through ok, so why are you coming after me?'

Ryan and Jane looked at each other puzzled.

'You must be confusing us with someone else, we're not the bad guys here, I work for British intelligence and my partner works for Interpol.'

'Shit!' he said.

'Shit exactly, I'm going to give you one chance to tell me the details of the last container that you helped them with, I need its number and I need it now.'

'I can't, they will kill me,' he said.

'I'll kill you if you don't tell me.' Ryan replied.

The man looked beat, so Ryan changed his tactics.

'Look, to be honest we don't really care about what you've been doing for them in the past and how much money you have made from them, we won't take this any further if you tell me that container number, and it better be the truth.'

'I'm not sure, you don't know what these people are capable of.'

'I think we do,' replied Ryan.

'If I speak, they will come for me, they know where I live, they know who my family are.'

'If you tell us what we need to know, we can help you, we can protect you and your family.'

'Do I have your word?'

'You have my word.'

Chapter 66

Ryan was cold, almost freezing, but he couldn't feel it, not really. The last eleven hours from when they eventually got the container number from the customs guy, had ended up with him lying on the roof of an abandoned factory building in central Scotland. He checked his watch, it was 4:06 a.m. — he was relaxed and waiting, same as he had been four days ago in Amsterdam.

***

The first thing they had done after getting the number from Graeme was to drive back to the customs office; they spoke with the same woman at the counter from earlier who fetched her supervisor, but all he could tell them was that the container had boarded the ferry and had passed through customs in Dover. The man explained to them that from there it would be moved onto a local haulage company who would then handle the paperwork and its tracking.

When they left the office, Ryan contacted Michael who was still in Rotterdam with Ryan's father. He told him about the customs guy and how they had got the container number from him, he then explained that the container had crossed through British customs with no problems. Michael said he would speak to the London office and try to find the haulage company handling the container. He had told Ryan to stay put for now while he tried to arrange transport to Britain.

They sat in the car and waited; Jane was thinking about what to do next. She didn't think her boss would be happy with her heading to Britain after everything that had gone on, and being honest with herself, she knew

Ryan should carry on alone. Ryan was thinking of ways he could get to Britain and considered checking the next ferry crossing when Michael phoned him back ten minutes after hanging up. He told him that with help from the French intelligence agency there was a plane sitting on a runway at Calais Dunkerque airfield which was only a ten-minute drive from where they were. He had decided that Leeds airport was as central as they could get in Britain and so he arranged for the plane to take him there, Ryan agreed.

Ryan drove and Jane explained on the way how she couldn't go with him, she told him she wanted to see it through to the end, but she really had to report back to head office with everything that had gone on, from the incident in their Dortmund office, to what had happened to Klass in Düsseldorf. Ryan understood and didn't protest, all he was focused on was reaching Britain and catching Sonny.

They carried on in silence until they reached the airfield. It was a small place but even so, they had to be checked and cleared before being let through. Ryan passed Jane the car keys when they got out before kissing her, the way he had wanted to the first time he met her in the bar, they kissed for a long time, wrapped in each other's arms. Ryan pulled away and told her he would call when he got the chance, Jane smiled and watched as he boarded the plane, it was a small four-seater and Ryan was the only passenger. He strapped himself in and watched from the window as Jane turned the car around and drove away.

The flight took one hour fifteen minutes and was less than enjoyable, visibility was low, and the thick clouds made the journey uncomfortable with turbulence. Although it was fairly quick it was still over an hour that he had no access to his phone and couldn't communicate with Michael.

When it finally landed however, he checked his phone again and he knew Michael had been busy. There were six messages from him, but instead of listening to them all he called him back. Michael had managed to enforce some pressure on the officer who was in charge of Graeme, mainly due to the fact that one of his men had been taking drug money to ensure shipments filled with drugs were passing through customs without being searched. He gave Michael the name of the haulage company that was dealing with the container in Britain that they believed Sonny to be in. Michael had called them to ask them a few questions, nothing that would make them wary and without revealing his purpose.

Meanwhile he had arranged for two of his men from the London office to make their way down to the haulage company itself. After the original resistance and with some gentle persuasion they found out that the container was still hitched with the original truck and the original driver who had brought it over — he was going to make the delivery in Britain himself. So as far as the haulage company were concerned, all they had to do was process the paperwork and make a note of the seal number and the license plate number.

The backshift worker at the haulage company's name was Barry, he was nervous and, in the end, realised he had no choice but to tell them what he knew. He started with bringing up the tracking system on his computer, he clicked on a small picture of a truck that brought up its information. It showed that at just after 8 p.m. the previous night it passed customs in Dover and began heading north soon after. The driver had called in to say that there was no need to stop, it was only making one delivery and he wanted to get there before sunrise and to miss the traffic, which was common from companies overseas. The downside to that was the haulage company didn't know exactly where the container was headed, but Barry said he could make an educated guess, and at this point Michael didn't have too many other options so he had to trust him. Barry explained that the company who belonged to this truck only made deliveries to three different addresses, and this had been the case for the last four years.

He brought up the three locations on his screen from previous invoices and checked them against the current location of the container now. The first address was in south London and by looking at the tracker he had already passed there, a few hours ago.

The second was in the north of Liverpool and the third was in central Scotland. They flicked back onto the tracking system and saw that the truck was sixty miles north of the junction for the Liverpool address, which meant that Barry was almost positive it was heading for Scotland. One of the men from the London office contacted Michael straight away and told him what they found out and what Barry thought might be the location of the container. Michael was glad that choosing to land the plane at Leeds airport could maybe pay off. He then arranged for a car to be waiting for Ryan when he got off the plane.

Ryan had listened intently to all the details Michael was telling him as he waited in line to reach the terminal. After he passed through passport control, he picked up the keys to a brand-new Jaguar s-type saloon car and typed in the post-code of the possible location into the cars satellite navigation system. He then pulled out of the airport and headed west onto the M6 motorway, and north, for Scotland. Judging by the current location of the container and where he was now, he knew he should reach the address before the container did.

Chapter 67

Michael, along with Ryan's father, had decided that the best course of action was to get Ryan there as soon as possible so they could hopefully have eyes on Sonny, if he was inside. Michael had dispatched backup but knew they wouldn't arrive until after 6 a.m. at the earliest. So, Ryan had to make sure if he located Sonny that he could not lose him, at any cost, and wait until back up had arrived, which Ryan understood.

The map on the cars screen had told Ryan that the location was halfway between Glasgow and Edinburgh, just off the M8 motorway that connected the two cities, and it would take him another three hours until he reached it.

He found out that the factory had been abandoned a little more than ten years ago and used to make airplane engines. The company had relocated to America and the building had lay empty ever since. The site itself was huge but the factory was now derelict and starting to rot. Ryan had managed to download an overhead image of it on his phone which gave him an idea of the layout and the best way to access it. He thought this would be on foot, it was roughly two miles through a heavily wooded area, and he didn't want to risk coming in from the main road and being spotted.

He cut off the M74 motorway onto the M73 then across onto the M8. He stayed on it until the sat nav told him to take the next exit, which he did. He came off the junction road and spotted the small access road he had found on the screen earlier. He parked the car far enough into it to avoid being seen. He then took out a black jacket and black woolen hat from the back seat and put them both on before making his way into the woods.

He reached the outskirts of the factory after thirty

minutes and found a spiral staircase that must have been used as a fire exit which was next to the main entrance. He climbed up to the first level — from there he was able to lift himself up and over a dividing wall and onto the roof. It took him a few minutes to find his equipment as it was pitch black. Lying out on the floor was a base sheet with a fleece lined cover on top, it was sitting behind his rifle that had already been set up for him, the same as it was in the hotel back in Amsterdam.

Once he had found the derelict building online, he messaged the details to Michael, who had arranged for a local desk officer in Edinburgh to get the rifle to the location and have it set up.

The rifle was placed on top of a small ledge at the edge of the building, he kneeled on the cover before lying down and getting into position. He nestled his shoulder in against the handle, it was cold on his cheek, and put his eye to the scope, it was pointing at a small warehouse 300 yards further up on the other side of the road. The view he had of it was good, as good as he would get from a safe distance; he could see the full shutter door and the entire front side. The only problem he could think of was when the container backed in, he wouldn't be able to see into the back of it. The lights inside were on but he hadn't seen any movement as of yet.

**

Ryan checked his watch again, it was now 4:17 a.m. he knew the container should arrive between 4 – 4:30 a.m. without any delays or stops. He closed his eyes; the cold was stinging them even though there wasn't a breath of wind. He lay there waiting and listening and then he heard it, the roar of a large truck engine no more than a mile away, he opened his eyes and felt a rush of adrenalin.

The truck was coming from behind his left shoulder, it must have taken the same route as he did. The noise got louder as it got closer and Ryan looked over the edge of the building as it passed by, it indicated left and pulled into the warehouse car park. He put his eye on the scope again to see it reversing up to the shutter door which was now opening.

Ryan saw inside the warehouse for the first time, it was brightly lit, on the far wall he could see lines of tyres stacked on blue racking, similar to the ones back in Rotterdam. The middle of the warehouse looked empty, possibly space made for the tyres to be unloaded from the container, he thought. The container was now being guided back by a worker who had come out and stopped it only a few feet into the warehouse. When the truck came to a stop there was seven other men who appeared from inside and approached the rear of the container. One of the men cut a plastic seal from the back doors with a pair of bolt cutters and another swung open the huge doors. Two men then lifted themselves up into it and a few seconds later tyres began rolling out and bouncing onto the warehouse floor.

Ryan knew that from Graeme, in Calais, Sonny would have locked himself in a small compartment that had been built at the front of the container. This meant that all the tyres had to be unloaded before he could get out, that's if he hadn't stopped already and got away, or if this was even the right container.

***

Sonny was sore, tired, and chilled to the bone and even though he had been pissing in plastic bottles for eighteen hours, he was happy. The truck had stopped, and he heard the seal being cut and the doors being opened. He sat up, Clarke had told him he had organised for there to be plenty of workers in the warehouse to get the tyres unloaded and get him out quickly, but Sonny knew that still meant at least another two hours, all he could do was wait.

Chapter 68

It had been one hour and fifty minutes since the container backed up and the men had started to unload it. To keep his mind alert, Ryan had thought about a lot of different things. He thought about Jane and Klass and hoped she managed to sort things out with her boss. He thought about his father, that he hadn't seen in nearly twenty years — who had turned out to be his boss and had been for many years without him knowing. He realised then that his father must have been the one who made sure he kept his job with the agency after his old unit had been investigated.

But mostly he thought about his mother. He tried his best to remember her and not just from photos, he was sure he could, he wished he had known more about her and could have spent more time with her and saw how much she had loved him. When he started to get angry thinking about the way she had died and by someone from her own family, who she'd trusted, he stopped himself, refocused and concentrated on the job he was there to do. He still hadn't heard any sirens or if any back up had arrived, but he wasn't phoning Michael now, they would just have to trust him. He had his father's words ringing in his ear about the importance of this man being brought to justice.

He took his eye from the scope, it was minus two degrees, and he was starting to shake a little, he had been on the roof for nearly two hours. He stretched out both his arms to get the blood flowing and looked up at the sky. It was threatening, as if at any moment it would fall, engulfing everything and everyone. It was forecast to snow but as of yet, it had relented.

A noise from up ahead made him quickly check through the scope again, the stream of tyres had stopped.

Someone jumped down from the back of the container, but it wasn't Sonny, they walked over to the corner and grabbed a set of ladders and leant them against the back of it. A minute passed, then another, Ryan stayed alert and focused, he could feel his heart beating in his chest.

Then a foot appeared on the top step, it was all Ryan could see at first, then the other foot, taking it slow, maybe stiff from being cramped up in a tight space, he thought. The figure stepped down another step, then another, until he stood on the concrete floor. Ryan still couldn't see his face yet, because of the angle, they paused for a second then started walking out and around to the side of the container.

They then stopped at the entrance to the warehouse, and he finally saw his face. Ryan was now staring at the man he had been chasing all over Europe for the last four days.

It was Sonny. His uncle. His Father's brother. His mother's killer.

He watched as he stretched his arms into the air and yawned.

Ryan knew what he had to do now.

But just then something caught his eye. A small white speck through the lens, then another, he didn't want to pull back from the scope, not now, but he had to. He looked up, the clouds were almost touching his head, the sky had relented for almost four days, but now it had let go.

Ryan smiled and put his eye back to the scope. Sonny was still in his sights, he hadn't moved. It was only the specks of white he could see floating past the lens that were moving now.

He watched as Sonny took in a big, deep breath. At the same time Ryan took a long breath out and steadied himself.

Silence.
Then he pulled the trigger.
At last.
A falling of Snow.

About The Author

Scott Carlin is from Scotland and lives with his family in a small village between Glasgow and Edinburgh. He started expressing his creative side in his teenage years, writing songs and performing live with his band.

He has always enjoyed reading crime thriller novels and after a few years began to write his debut novel 'A falling of Snow,' published by Blossom Spring Publishing.

Scott's interests outside of work include traveling, which has allowed him to experience different cultures, foods and support his creativity, enabling him to incorporate his encounters into his stories. Scott also enjoys engaging in a wide range of sports including golf and football, he loves music and taking long walks in the countryside with his much loved springer spaniel, Poppy.

www.blossomspringpublishing.com

Printed in Great Britain
by Amazon